Praise for Anne Charnock's
A Calculated Life

"[*A Calculated Life*] is lovingly crafted, beautifully made in the economical, expert way a piece of Arts and Crafts furniture is made—pure lines, and perfectly suited to its intended purpose . . . Anne Charnock is clearly a gifted and sensitive author of acute intelligence, writing science fiction of a kind—quiet, intense, thoughtful—we could do with more of."
—Nina Allan, winner of the 2013 BSFA Best Short Fiction Award for *Spin*

"Charnock is a subtle worldbuilder . . . For readers who want a smart, subtle exploration of human emotion and intelligence, this is an excellent choice."
—Alix E. Harrow, *Strange Horizons*

"A very noteworthy book . . . What Charnock shares with Philip K. Dick is the ability to write unease . . . She has fascinating, complex things to say about work, sex, family and hope."
—Adam Roberts, author of *Jack Glass*, winner of the 2012 BSFA Best Novel Award

"This story puts us inside one of the most interesting perspectives I've encountered in recent fiction. Jayna's perspective is so unique that I would happily have followed her anywhere, and, as a consequence, the cleverness of this plot almost snuck up on me. A smart, stylish, emotionally compelling book with literary richness and sci-fi smarts."
—Susan DeFreitas, author of *Hot Season*

"Charnock [is] an astute observer herself, [and] what results is an inquiry into feminism and society that will make the reader truly pause to compare their own experiences and perceptions."

—*Speculiction*

Praise for Anne Charnock's
Sleeping Embers of an Ordinary Mind

Included in the *Guardian*'s Best Science
Fiction and Fantasy Books of 2015

"Anne Charnock's *Sleeping Embers of an Ordinary Mind* is an expert braiding together of past, present and future that puts a fifteenth-century Italian female artist centre stage to say penetrating things about womanhood, creativity and history."

—Adam Roberts, the *Guardian*

"*Sleeping Embers of an Ordinary Mind* is certainly one of 2015's tip-top releases in science fiction."

—*Speculiction*

"This quiet, lovely and exquisitely crafted novel is itself a masterclass in composition . . . As in her debut novel, *A Calculated Life*, the clarity and refined elegance of Charnock's prose is a significant achievement."

—Nina Allan, winner of the 2013 BSFA Best Short Fiction Award for *Spin*

"The feminist elements of *Sleeping Embers of an Ordinary Mind* are elusively contradictory, so much like life!, making this one of those thinking books— the kind with embers smoldering until a second visit. I look forward to more from Anne Charnock.

—*From Couch to Moon*

"The centuries-spanning story gives the mystery an epic feel."

—*Kirkus Reviews*

DREAMS
BEFORE
THE ## START
OF ## TIME

DREAMS BEFORE THE START OF TIME

ANNE CHARNOCK

Text copyright © 2017 by Anne Charnock
All rights reserved.

No part of this book may be reproduced, or stored in a retrieval system, or transmitted in any form or by any means, electronic, mechanical, photocopying, recording, or otherwise, without express written permission of the publisher.

Published by 47North, Seattle

www.apub.com

Amazon, the Amazon logo, and 47North are trademarks of Amazon.com Inc. or its affiliates.

ISBN-13: 9781503934726
ISBN-10: 1503934721

Cover design by David Drummond

Printed in the United States of America

For Adam and Robert

CONTENTS

PART ONE

2034

THE APPLE TREE

August

This year's crop of apples is so poor that Betty Matheson counts the overnight windfalls when she opens her bedroom shutters each morning. Today, she looks down on the gravel path and sees a split apple at exactly the point where she expected to see one; she heard the crunch of that singular windfall just after dawn. As a rule, she collects the apples, or apple, before breakfast. That is, before too much damage is inflicted by stabbing blackbirds and burrowing wasps.

In years gone by, the tree was so burdened that apples thumped down on the lawn throughout the night. Back then, she discarded any split apples, any apples with a bruise, and all the small apples that, she convinced herself, were too fiddly to peel. When she'd filled her two-handled blue bucket with near-flawless windfalls, she felt she'd met her responsibility to the tree. The rest had to go.

She wonders how such a perfectly shaped and healthy apple tree could have caused her so much stress. Whenever she went away from home, she implored neighbours to collect the windfalls. "Or take whatever you can reach on the tree." She felt embarrassed, offering apples from the bough *after* offering the windfalls. But surely it made sense to everyone to take the windfalls first.

As it happened, most of her neighbours had their own apple trees, so Betty inevitably returned home to a war zone of fallen apples—cracked and speckled brown with fungal eruptions. She can't erase the memory—the scars and the rotting.

These years most of the apples are small, and there's no surplus.

Five small red apples hang high in the tree's crown, too high for Betty to reach even at a stretch from a ladder. She hopes they'll have a soft landing.

Nothing is as it should be. Her husband dead, despite being five years her junior. That wasn't supposed to happen. She never imagined herself as the one left behind. And Aiden, her son, so loving. So loving, but . . . "Damn it, Aiden," she says through her teeth. She imagines herself placing her arms around the trunk of the apple tree. Her caress morphs into a bear hug. She tears the tree from the ground, roots and all, and she thrashes the canopy against the ground.

Still in her pyjamas, Betty turns from the window and pads across to her walk-in wardrobe. Reaching into the far right corner behind her nana's red fox-fur coat, she allows familiar thoughts to surface: Come the apocalypse, she'll be glad she hung on to her nana's furs. Who on earth will have *any* qualms about fur when no one has central heating, when survivors are marauding, scavenging for out-of-date tins of baked beans?

Betty has carried this conviction for thirty years.

From behind the fur coat, she pulls out a long, soft case, drags the zip from top to bottom and pulls out the air rifle. She takes a tin of pellets from the side pocket.

She walks back to her bedroom, throws open the windows, breaks the rifle and loads a pellet. She aims at the topmost red apple and fires. Reloads, aims and fires. Reloads, aims and fires.

※

The apple tree has stood, ready, for so long. A decade ago, the tree surgeon came to cut away the low branches and tidy up the crown. Betty and her husband tied string around the branches to mark the line of the cuts. They wanted a three-foot lateral that could take a child's swing. As for the other low branches, the surgeon said they should be cut in line with the trunk, but Betty and her husband insisted he cut them proud of the trunk. Otherwise, a child would find it too difficult to climb the tree.

And now Aiden's girlfriend is having a baby. He came up last weekend, and when he told Betty the news, she assumed, as anyone would—after all, he'd made a special effort to visit—that the baby was *his*. Aiden recoiled as Betty clapped her palms together.

"No!" he said. "I'm sorry, that *isn't* what I've come to tell you. It's not mine."

She still had her palms together when he moved from the armchair to sit next to her on the sofa. "Millie wanted a baby, but the time's not right for me. I'm not ready. In fact, Millie and I are taking a break."

"What do you mean?"

"We're still best friends. You *know*, Mum, that's how it's always been with Millie and me. We're not into the physical side of things. I keep trying to explain—"

"But she's your girlfriend. You live together."

"Well, not any more. That's what I've come to tell you—I've handed in my notice at work; I've decided I want to travel."

Holy Mother of God. He wants to travel! "But who's the father if it's not you?"

"She's going solo. Donor sperm."

At that point, Betty felt like heaving. She looked out of the window as though seeing her garden for the first time; the world had become unrecognizable. "Donor sperm? Why didn't she *use yours*? Why does she want a baby with a stranger?"

Looking back, she knows this upset him. He didn't say anything at the time, remained calm, but the deep crease between his brows gave the lie. He stood up and walked to the kitchen, filled the kettle with water. She realizes now that her remark had been disrespectful—of him *and* of Millie. She'll be more careful in future. But saints alive! He surely deserved it.

Aiden returned to the sofa with two mugs of tea. He said, "Listen, Mum, it's still exciting. She reckons it's a boy, and she's chosen a name. She's going to call him Rudy. And guess what? I'm so chuffed. I'm going to be the child's godfather."

Betty made him his favourite dinner that evening. She switched on the outdoor lights set into the lawn around the apple tree. She noticed for the first time that the light was a cold white light.

She asked him—over beef, Yorkshire pudding and homemade horseradish sauce—how Millie would cope looking after a baby on her own. Had he any idea how difficult it was going to be for her? And how would she manage for money? Had she worked it all out?

He shrugged and said it wasn't his job to micromanage her life, but obviously, they had talked about it. In any case, her parents had already stepped in to help out; they'd stumped up the money so she could buy a flat. And Millie had asked Robyn, her older sister, to move in with her. "Millie and her sister are close. I think they want to live together permanently."

"Permanently?" Betty was incredulous.

He didn't answer.

She said, "What happens when you get back? Will you start over with Millie?"

"Possibly. I might be in another relationship by then, but if I'm ready for fatherhood, I could have a baby with Millie. If that's what she wants. If she'd prefer to know the father."

Betty wondered at his weary smile as he said, "I'd do anything for her, Mum. I love her to bits."

He didn't say one word of thanks for the dinner, as Betty recalls, which wasn't *at all* like him. He left a slice of perfectly cooked beef on his plate, and he didn't even touch the second of his Yorkshire puddings.

Ж

Betty knows she shouldn't shoot from the bedroom window; a pellet might zing through the beech hedge into her neighbour's garden. Nevertheless, she loads the air rifle once again and takes one more shot at the topmost apple. It thumps to the ground and splits. She leans the air rifle against the windowsill. She wishes she had one of those big American shotguns with a loud, convincing pump action.

FIRST CONTACT

"Millie Dack, sit back down! You're not buying a round if you're only having tomato juice," says Toni. "Same again, everyone?"

"Finish the story first, Toni," says Atticus.

"I'll leave you in suspenders," she says.

They all titter. Toni points in turn to the glasses on the table and raises her eyebrows at each of her friends, prompting a decision. Dry white for Alice. A pint of London Pride for Alice's workmate. Red for Atticus, who says, "The French merlot, not the bloody awful rioja they serve here."

"I'll switch to sparkling water," says Millie.

"Good for you!" says Toni. She beams a smile. "Feeling okay?"

"Not great. I'm losing the morning sickness, but I'm tired out. I won't be staying long."

Toni reaches out and strokes her hair. "You're looking well, kiddo." And she slips away to the bar.

Millie loves her friend's travel stories; they're so vivid. Whenever Millie recalls them, she has to remind herself she wasn't actually there. She has never been Toni's travelling companion. She likes the idea of travel, but the thought of packing a suitcase—choosing which linen shorts and slinky dresses to take, which sandals and jerseys to leave behind—generates a whirlwind of uncertainty. And she doesn't care for strong sunshine, so she ignores beach holidays on any list she happens to peruse—"Best Weekend Getaways," "Bucket-List Destinations." Nothing truly tempts her. It's a mystery to Millie how the world is populated with billions of souls consumed by lifelong wanderlust. She's the odd one out, preferring to stay close to home. So far no one has noticed this minor quirk. Even Aiden never commented. She allowed him to believe she was hellbent on saving money to pay off her student loans. Quite apart from her packing dilemmas and her dislike of sunshine, she can't face the hassle of delayed flights, missed connections, insect bites. Whereas Toni Munroe takes it all in her stride—she views the accumulation of daily dramas as the signature of any adventure.

Toni is halfway through the tale of her latest travel disaster, and Millie senses a classic in the making. What was that ancient silent film serial, she wonders? *The Perils of Pauline.* That was it. Toni attracts peril. Or maybe she travels more frequently than most, so she's bound to experience more calamity.

Toni's story so far: some guy took her suitcase off the airport carousel and rushed away into Prague. She knew it was a guy because she found herself in a deserted baggage hall with *his* suitcase—the same model—with a luggage label stating *Mr. E. Strickland.* "It's the last time I travel with a black suitcase," she said. This Strickland guy had wrapped a strip of fluorescent green tape around the bag's handle. "Can you believe it? He still took my suitcase, which"—she threw her hands out in recalled disbelief—"had *gold twine* around its handle. How could he mistake gold twine for green tape? And I had a blue club card attached to my case, which he didn't."

"So you were stuck with some slummer's baggage," Alice said. "The indignity."

Toni traipsed to the customer services desk at the far end of the baggage hall. The assistant told her, "Don't worry, Ms. Munroe. This happens all the time. We'll get your bag back to you within two hours. Mr. Strickland will come straight back to the airport. It always happens." Except, the assistant evidently copied the address down incorrectly from Toni's information sheet, laid out under her nose on the high counter; four hours later the bag hadn't arrived.

And now Millie and her friends wait for the rest of the tale. Atticus helps Toni carry the drinks from the bar to the large oak table they've commandeered by the window of the Hermit's Cave pub.

"Go on, then," says Alice. "Finish the story."

"So, I'm on the phone in my rented flat. The airport staff tell me the suitcase has already been delivered to my address."

"Oh shit," says Alice.

"I know. I get them to repeat all the information on the manifest, and that's when I realize it's been delivered to the wrong building in my street, the wrong street number. I dash out to find number twenty-five—it's half a block away. Huge austere edifice. Very Eastern European, enormous double-entrance doors, dirty windows, no lights on inside and an entrance buzzer with a small nameplate . . ."

Her friends are leaning in, captivated.

"It's the Kyrgyzstan consulate. Un-bloody-believable. Completely shut for the weekend by this point."

Millie can see that Toni's predicament is funny only in hindsight—surely she was sweating buckets.

"I pressed the buzzer. No one answered. So I banged on the doors with my fist, but I hardly made a sound—the doors were massive. God knows what they made of the surveillance footage when they came in on Monday. I phoned the airport, again, and they kept me on hold while they checked. Lo and behold, the courier reports that my case is still in his van. And there's me trying to break down the consulate door. Eventually—the next day around noon—my case arrives. I honestly expected to receive a note of apology and a bottle of wine from Mr. Strickland. But nothing. Nada."

"You knew his name though."

"Yeah. It was tempting to track him down. However, you *can* start a war that way."

A competition ensues over who has a better lost-luggage story.

Three of Alice's work colleagues arrive. Toni wanders over to join the new contingent at the end of the bar. Atticus makes a move to join them, but then settles back in his seat. After a couple of minutes, he feigns nonchalance and drifts across to stand beside Toni. He takes a swig of his beer; he doesn't join the conversation. Millie notices Atticus place his hand at Toni's elbow. Millie guesses he'd prefer to have Toni all to himself—but he's caught Toni midflow in conversation. She glances at him. The smile she offers is fleeting, keeps him in a holding pattern— Not yet, not now, she seems to say.

As Millie drains her glass, the ice cubes slip and crash into her teeth. She flinches, taken by surprise, and tears flood her eyes. She's on a knife edge these days, so emotional. Unless it's tiredness—she should go home, get an early night. But she can't summon the strength to stand up from the table. Another ten minutes.

There's an explosion of laughter. As it subsides, Toni faces Atticus. She puts her arms around his waist, pulls him in for a full on-the-mouth kiss. Millie tries not to watch, but it's difficult to look away; she's addicted to a game of compare and contrast. Aiden and she were affectionate with one another, and pretty demonstrative with it too. But not so . . . *hungry* as Toni appears to be with Atticus. Did Aiden need more than she could offer, more than he was prepared to admit? Is a break-up inevitable when her "no libido" meets a "low libido"? Millie reckons she'd kidded herself all along—she and Aiden would never have worked out, not in the long term. She won't make that mistake again.

It's no use. It's time to go. Millie picks up her coat from the next chair. She takes a deep breath, exhales slowly, and at the end of her breath, she feels a prod. Like the blunt end of a pencil poking her from the inside. The baby moved! She stares down at herself, unblinking. This isn't how she imagined *first contact*—of all places, in a pub. Instinctively, she places her palm on the side of her belly. She feels the prod again. She looks up and waves to catch Toni's attention.

When Toni glances over, she instantly reads Millie's pose and rushes across the pub.

"I felt the baby! First time," says Millie.

"Let me feel."

Millie takes Toni's hand and flattens her palm against the bump. And they wait. Then comes the baby's third prod, and Toni's glee. "Oh my God!" she whispers. "Is this early?"

"Late end of normal. Twenty-four weeks. I've been a bit anxious. You know . . . waiting for it."

"You should have told me."

Millie laughs. "Doesn't matter now."

"You know what this means? If it's a girl, you'll have to name her after me. I felt her first."

"That's how it works, is it?" She laughs again.

"I'll be the best fake auntie."

Millie pats Toni's hand. "I'm sure it's a boy. And let's face it, you'll be the worst influence of all."

"Hey. We know who'll take that trophy. Your hippie sister."

Toni puts her arms around Millie's shoulders and gives her a gentle hug, as though Millie were breakable, as though she were a child. Millie murmurs, "I'm going. I'm knackered."

"I'll walk you to the bus."

"Don't bother, Toni. It's been lovely to see everyone."

"I don't mind. I'm happy to walk with you."

"Please, don't. You're having fun."

X

As Millie leaves the Hermit's Cave for the number 412 bus, she casts a glance through the engraved pub window and sees that Toni has rejoined the group at the table. Millie imagines her group of friends frozen in the moment—rendered conspiratorial in a staged photograph, with all eyes on

Toni's animated face. The backdrop to the photograph: the timeless setting of the Hermit's Cave. There's nothing architectural to pin the scene to a specific period within the past two hundred years. Dimpled pint glasses hang from pegs above the polished bar. The oak table has a patina of accumulated stains from cold drinks set down without beer mats. It wouldn't surprise her if a serving wench wandered over and deposited a hunk of spit-roasted lamb on the table. Millie pauses and raises her hand. She beams a smile when Toni, and then Atticus and Alice, look up and wave back.

How does Toni do that? Whenever Millie sees Toni in a group photo, it's as though Toni has cast a spell on the photographer: she looks natural, unforced. Most likely, the person taking the photo waited until Toni looked good, had the perfect authentic smile—not a pasted-on smile, not a smile to order. It's as though the photographer doesn't check if anyone else is ready for the shot. Millie wonders if she can learn how to do that. Is she missing some essential magnetism? Would that actually fit with her lack of libido?

She sits on the narrow red bench in the bus shelter. The 412 is due in eleven minutes according to the overhead display. She messages her sister: *Baby moved!!!* Robyn replies: *Hurry. I want to feel! xxx*. Millie replies: *Waiting for bus. Home in 30 xxx*.

Although Millie put no pressure on Robyn, she's relieved her sister moved in with her last week. It makes so much sense, though she wonders if Robyn will regret her decision one day; family life—the routine that a baby forces on a household, plus the play mats, toys, prams, not to mention the disturbed sleep—may prove suffocating. Millie won't blame Robyn if it doesn't work out, but her sister's presence in the house has already eased her many apprehensions about the future: Will she cope with the baby? Will she feel lonely?

Growing up, Robyn was the laid-back, sunny sibling, though this never seemed to win over their parents. Old family photographs exposed the pretence that the Drs. Dack held all three children in equal favour: it's clear to Millie that her brother, Bryan, the eldest of the three, came first in more ways than one.

When Millie visited home last, she skimmed through the albums, and with motherhood approaching, she selected photos to frame—photos of herself as a baby, of her sister and brother, of her grandparents in their prime. Millie couldn't find a single photo in which she took centre stage. Even in a rare photo of Millie sitting in her mother's lap—no other siblings in sight—she fails to grab the camera's attention. It's her glamorous mother in a wide-brimmed hat who fixed the photographer's gaze. It looks as though her mother was showing off her new hat rather than her child. That's how Millie reads it, but she could be wrong. Yet even in the photos showing all three children, she's never the focus. It's her brother, Bryan, always. Millie—to a lesser extent her sister—is invariably not quite *present*. She's partly obscured, or looking away from the lens, or caught with a deathly half-blink of the eyes.

Still, framed up and set out along the shelves and mantelpiece in her sitting room, these family photographs charm Millie. She's surprised how they've transformed her flat into a home. It's an unexpected spin-off. Her sole intention was to look for similarities between the baby and her family. Even if the baby doesn't look like her, it will be comforting if he looks like one of her siblings. Next time she's home, she'll nab photos of her other relatives.

She recalls one sepia photo, in the oldest black-leaved album, of a starchy elderly couple. No one in the family can identify either the woman or the man. Looks early twentieth century, possibly late nineteenth, but it's not the usual posed photograph of that era, shot against a painted backdrop in a studio. However, both figures are well dressed. Millie reckons that someone in the family, or a friend, bought an early camera. Millie can imagine this friend, or whoever, calling by after Sunday church, and saying, Come on. Let's have a photograph of you both! Stand in the back yard. It's too dark inside the house. Maybe that Sunday, he (and Millie assumes the photographer was a he) visited all his friends in the vicinity and shot a whole film. Did he develop the film himself and give the prints as gifts? More likely, he hoped to start a small business—a new cottage industry. How many frames were on a roll of film? Had roll film been invented? Or did the camera capture an image on a single photographic plate?

In this particular photograph, the couple are posed in the paved, grim back yard of a small house, a Victorian miner's house most likely. This couple—they could be man and wife or brother and sister—they look worried. The woman looks particularly dour. People in those days hadn't learned the art of self-presentation. The man looks sixty or so—upright, solid build, neat white beard. Handsome, though severe. Whoever he is—now lost in time, lost in space—he's the spitting image of Millie's brother, Bryan. It gives her the creeps that no one knows this man's name, or how he's connected to their family, yet her brother's face stares out.

⋊

An elderly man and woman—in their sixties, at least—sit down hand in hand beside Millie in the bus shelter. Millie likes seeing people holding hands. She assumes the couple are on a second or third marriage. It seems unlikely they'd still be holding hands if they'd married forty years ago. Anyway, they might not be married, she muses. Just because they're old, it doesn't mean they're the marrying type. Not all old people are like her mother and father.

She cringes because she can't dissociate the word *father* from the stupid comment her own father made when she and Aiden started dating. She'd tried in the past to explain about her sexuality, or lack thereof, and when she told him about Aiden—explaining that Aiden wasn't fussed about sex either—her father said, at his most affected, "At least you're not gay any more." Treating her as trivial and dissing her ex-girlfriend in one fell swoop. Millie was stunned. She couldn't look at his eyes, only at his nose, and she wondered why her mother hadn't told him to trim his nostril hairs. This tangential thought seemed to defuse her anger, and she feels proud that she mustered a retort: "You know, you actually thought that aloud." She didn't bother to explain any further. He wouldn't have been interested. But from then on her parents started to refer to Aiden as "Millie's friend" or "Millie's companion."

It also irks Millie—the irritations cascade once she starts thinking of her parents' shortcomings—that her mother and father, both hospital consultants, have no conception of how other professionals operate. They have no respect, put brutally, for any talents other than the diagnosis of ailments, and the dexterous invasion of the body to cure said ailments. The fact that Millie passed the Civil Service exams appeared to be of no interest to them. She and her sister didn't choose medicine. And Millie detects in her parents a gut-punching disappointment; they see themselves as shooting stars while their offspring aim low, for downright ordinariness. Yet Millie considers her own work in recent years—briefing departmental and even cabinet ministers—as equally worthwhile despite her relative invisibility. She has considered hinting to her parents—it wouldn't be true—that she works within a special area of the Civil Service. She could intimate, for the hell of it, that she's involved in the secret services.

Of course, her relationships with her mother and father have changed since she became pregnant, and Millie is slowly adjusting to seeing her parents, her father in particular, in new guises. In fact, she occasionally thinks of them now as *mum and dad*, as she used to.

Her parents were dismayed about her pregnancy, bemused about her decision to go solo, but perfectly unconcerned that Aiden had moved on. To Millie, it seems they've rewritten the narrative they present to the world concerning their younger daughter: *now* she's a capable, independent woman with a guaranteed pension. However, Millie's interpretation is this: they like the idea of becoming grandparents; they look forward to discussing medical, pregnancy-related matters with their daughter; and they're relieved to avoid the nuisance of an underachieving son-in-law.

The bus arrives and she takes a seat downstairs. As the doors are about to close, a young man jumps aboard and swipes his pass. She assesses him, as she tends to assess most men of late. She wonders if *he* could be the sperm donor.

He fits the spec—looks smart, professional, intelligent. He climbs the spiral staircase to the upper deck. And once again she's prompted into a circular argument. Even if Aiden had agreed to father a child with her—after all, it's not as though they *never* had sex—she guesses she'd renege on her promise of "no strings attached." She'd try to forge a relationship between Aiden and the child, and she'd become resentful if he took her at her word and felt no obligation. Of course his mother, Betty, would dote on the child. Then Aiden would feel under even more pressure, if Betty tried to draw him in, which naturally she would do.

Again, she concludes she's better off going solo.

Much to Millie's surprise, her parents were galvanized into action once the shock wore off. Her mother declared, with the slightest crack in her voice, that *no daughter of hers* would have a baby while living in rented accommodation. Millie can't help but smirk; her parents' archaic attitudes played out, for once, to her benefit. They drew down a chunk from each of their pension pots so they could help her to buy a flat. And, knowing Millie had little spare time or energy, they offered to spearhead the property search. They approached that search as a military exercise—one that had to succeed before "B-Day," as they called it. Birth Day. Her mother said, "Mark an area on the map of London where you'd like to live, and leave the rest to us." And that, pretty much, was that. They found two properties they considered fit for their daughter. Millie viewed them and made her choice.

Millie hears the bell ring for the next bus stop. The fantasy sperm donor reappears from the upper deck and waits by the exit doors as the bus gently glides to a halt. The doors hiss open, he looks over his shoulder. He must have felt her eyes boring into him. Their eyes meet, and then he steps off. The doors hiss shut.

Well, that's the end of him.

She's on her own. But soon there'll be little Rudy.

SOMEONE TOTALLY RELIABLE, WITH BLUE EYES

Toni Munroe decides she'll pay the concierge to remove the mirrors from both bedrooms and the hallway. Two mirrors are more than sufficient in one flat—a mirror in the bathroom over the sink and a full-length mirror somewhere else, anywhere. She slouches towards the bathroom. It's ridiculous—seeing yourself at every turn.

She switches on the shower, and while the water is warming, she cleans her teeth. Another midweek drinking session. What was she thinking? At thirty-two years of age, she's getting too old for this. And she has two major deadlines this afternoon. At least she can work in her pyjamas. Eyes down, she avoids seeing the fallout from last night's excesses at the Hermit's Cave—bloaty eyelids, sagging cheeks. She won't look so bad after a shower.

Stepping into the shower cubicle, she reaches out and places her right palm on the medic console—she hates the damned thing. She hasn't checked her health status for well over a month, but now she wants to jolt herself. It's time to grow up. Flashing red text: *Alcohol Alert: Toni, do not ride your bicycle before 1500 hours.*

"Oh! That's really, really bad," she murmurs.

Then: *Drink plenty of water.* And then: *You are pregnant. Congratulations, Toni.*

"Fan. On." The steam begins to clear.

She sits naked on the bathtub's scroll top and stares at her wet footprints. Wet feet, dry feet. Knowing, not knowing. It's tempting to walk backwards through the bathroom and slip back between the sheets, start the day afresh.

She could terminate, straight away—today or tomorrow. "Christ. Which night was it?" she says under her breath. Since she last checked her health stats, she's stayed over with Atticus once or twice a week, possibly nine times in total. Her periods are never particularly regular, so, at worst, if she fell pregnant the first of those times—could be five or six weeks ago?

She looks up at her reflection in the mirror over the sink. "Jeez!" This is not how she planned it. She drags a towel around her shoulders and leans forward to rest her head on the sink rim. Yes, she wants a baby, but not with Atticus. She hardly knows him. She's not starting a baby by accident. It's just sex with Atticus. *Was.* She'll end it. Toni wants agreements in place before she ever starts a family. And she's sure there's a better guy out there, someone ready and eager for fatherhood, someone totally reliable, with . . . blue eyes?

※

The kitchen still reeks of fried eggs—her late-night supper. She can't think with a mess around her, so she wipes the scattered salt from the worktop and scrubs the congealed remains from her plate. Satisfied, she brews her tea, adds a drop of milk and sits at her breakfast bar. No music, no news bulletins; she sits quietly, sipping her tea. Toni knows she's in shock, but she can't stop herself chasing ahead. Her thoughts are scrambled. She won't tell anyone, not yet. She won't tell Atticus. Hell!

She can't not tell him. She should tell him and suggest a termination. He'd probably agree, or would he? Is he religious?

If she doesn't terminate, he might . . . She can't think straight. She places her hand on the baby-smooth skin of her stomach, slick with sweat. Atticus hasn't even met her dad. How would she break the news to him? What would her mum have said? Toni is on the verge of calling Millie, but changes her mind. How can she talk to Millie about an unwanted pregnancy?

She stands up from the bar stool and, on automatic, switches on her vintage coffee machine. That's her routine, a mug of tea followed by an espresso. For once, she doesn't refill the reservoir with fresh water—yesterday's will do. She watches the green light blink as the coils, or whatever, heat up. While she waits, she gazes at the three small paintings that sit on a shelf above the kitchen work surface.

She used to keep her collection of espresso cups on this shelf—she collects miniature cups and saucers on her travels; it gives her a fun personal quest when she visits any street market. But she relegated the cups and saucers to a cupboard when her dad gave her these paintings, a triptych. He came over on Toni's birthday, a couple of years ago, and said, "These paintings were always yours. You should have them here." For the previous twenty years, the paintings had sat on a kitchen shelf in their family home. Toni looks at them now and blinks away tears. Her dad is so thoughtful, and this is how she repays him.

He painted the pictures himself. They're oils, unframed—painted from photographs she snapped in China. She had joined her dad on a business trip after her mother died, a year after, in fact. The paintings show close-ups of carved graffiti—pale brown Chinese characters carved into green bamboo—which she discovered in a fairy-tale garden in Suzhou, the Master of the Nets Garden. She never had the graffiti translated; she wants the carvings to remain as mysterious as they seemed to her thirteen-year-old self. These days, the paintings remind her of her confusion back then, so soon after her mother's car accident.

21

Toni still feels she returned from China in a better state of mind—as though the onslaught of unfamiliar sights had rebooted her brain.

She glances down. The green light has stopped blinking. She takes the first cup at hand and makes a double espresso. As she takes her first sip, she wonders if pregnant women are supposed to cut down on caffeine. She can't recall Millie ordering a coffee recently.

It occurs to Toni that if she keeps the baby, Atticus might want to move in. She doesn't care for that idea, but then, if she doesn't let him move in, he might drift away; she'll be bringing up a baby on her own. In a knee-jerk, she calls the co-parenting agency, which she contacted a month ago when she was feeling particularly broody. She'd had lunch that day with Millie and was almost sick with envy over Millie's pregnancy. Toni didn't say anything to her friend, but personally she'd never opt for donor sperm—could be anybody's! Nice genes, never mind the sociopathic personality.

The agency receptionist picks up.

"Hi. My name's Toni Munroe. I'm considering co-parenting, and I have an appointment on Friday with the clinic's counsellor—

"No, I've no contract yet. I'm afraid I have to cancel—

"Yes, I know it's short notice, but something came up at work—

"I'm so sorry, I can't reschedule just yet—

"No, I haven't changed my mind. Leave it with me a few days—

"So sorry. Bye."

She hasn't moved from her bar stool. She slumps forward with her closed fists against her forehead and recalls the co-parenting advertisement, which she saw immediately after her lunch with Millie. It was a large poster that happened to face Toni as she waited on the platform for a Victoria line train. She was still thinking about Millie—her obvious delight at being pregnant—and no doubt that's why the advert snagged.

Toni felt embarrassed taking a photo of the contact details. So much so, she held her phone at waist height, angled up towards the advertisement, and took the shot while looking away.

YES, YOU CAN HAVE A CHILD WITHOUT A ROMANTIC RELATIONSHIP.
IF YOU ARE SINGLE, IF YOU ARE GAY, IF YOU ARE GENDER FLUID, SIGN UP
FOR OUR CO-PARENTING INTRODUCTION SERVICE!
CHOOSE YOUR CO-PARENT FROM OUR DATABASE—A SPECIAL **FOREVER**
FRIEND WHO IS EQUALLY KEEN TO BE A LOVING PARENT!
THOUSANDS OF HAPPY CHILDREN ARE NOW BEING RAISED BY
PLATONIC CO-PARENTS WHO **DON'T** LIVE UNDER THE SAME ROOF!
SHARE THE JOY, SHARE THE WORK

A forever friend? At the time, it sounded so much easier to Toni to find a forever friend than a forever boyfriend. Toni has already downloaded the forms—page after page of teasing blank boxes offering the giddying prospect of an ideal co-parent. Education, hobbies, cultural interests, eye colour, hair colour, physique, religion, politics. Oddly, nothing about attitudes to discipline. This particular omission has niggled her; it's the reason she hasn't ticked any boxes as yet. Imagine teaming up with a control freak.

Which prompts her to reassess Atticus. He seems pretty relaxed with life. She can't imagine him getting uptight. He must be reasonably intelligent too. But he's a damn football fanatic. She and Atticus have somehow bypassed the usual get-to-know-you stuff, which isn't surprising. He's a sex-buddy, basically, and it's working great; it's all she's wanted since her split with Freddie.

She inhales deeply, puffs out her cheeks and slowly releases her breath. Idiot. It's too late to ask Atticus the easy stuff—brothers and sisters, does he have any? Where did he study? So she shoots off a message:

Hi Alice, free to chat?
Not now, Toni. I'll call you back on lunch break. About?
Your friend. Atticus.
Ah!!!!!!!

Making his way through Camberwell to the elevated cycle route, Atticus O'Neill is pleased when the traffic lights change to red outside the Hermit's Cave pub. He can see the far end of the bar, where he stood last night with Toni and her friends—journos and teachers, a couple of city types. He didn't know them all. For most of the time, he felt on the periphery, whereas Toni, all evening, took centre stage during the best conversations—fast banter, laughter and in-jokes lost on him. He can't believe he's dating her. She could be *the one*. But then, she didn't stay over last night, mentioned early deadlines. An excuse? Or did he bang on too much about his footy team? Bored her rigid, probably.

He knows part of the reason he's attracted to her is that she owns her own flat. She's solvent. And he knows this reflects badly on him, but he's done his share of supporting other people, his parents. She might have a private income.

When they all left the pub last night, he felt a knot in his stomach. He wanted her to stay over. He wonders if she's backing off. And why hasn't she ever asked him over to her place?

A car honks. He looks up and sees the traffic lights changing from amber to red, again. "Shit," he says. He needs to snap out of it. He doesn't do daydreams.

⚹

Finally, Toni faces a mirror, swipes away the puffiness under her eyes with her forefingers. The effect is short-lived. She feels guilty about last night's boozing. She recalls that as she approached the Hermit's Cave, she promised herself she'd drink water from ten o'clock onwards, but she soon lost track of time. When the bell rang for last orders at eleven—she groans at the memory—she egged on her friends to have another round: "Well, I'm having a whisky for the road, so who's joining me?" If she tells her friends she's pregnant, they'll all remember that heavy midweek session.

Atticus is a nice name. She scratches her head. What on earth does it mean?

She sits at her admin desk, which is the messier of two desks that stand at right angles in her supposed living room-come-kitchen. The second desk, a Danish rosewood antique, is where she writes. And her designated relaxation space is a single armchair that's angled slightly away from her work area. Toni opens the forms from the co-parenting agency, but before inspecting them, she searches for boys' names.

Atticus: inhabitant of Attica. Um, boring. And more: *Atticus was a Roman man of letters who is reputed to be the first publisher because he directed his freed slave, Tiro, to copy Cicero's letters.* Still boring.

Back to the co-parenting forms. If she terminates her pregnancy, she could start afresh with someone on the database, start artificial insemination at the clinic with Mr. Right's cleaned-up sperm. If that doesn't work, she could begin IVF with Mr. Right's cleaned-up sperm. And if she's going to take that path, she wants the full monty—what the agency calls a fully refined search and matching service. What if there's no match for all her box ticks? It could be a con. She reckons the agency can offer only an approximate match. Whoever she settles on, she needs to be best buddies with him, because she could be meeting him every week for at least eighteen years—that is, if she goes ahead with this. There's a suspicion—it's stalking her—that if she's right-on politically correct when she ticks the boxes, she'll be matched to someone she can't abide.

She isn't bothered about sexual preference or religion, but she is concerned about his outlook on life, which might conceivably be genetic, at least in part. It's a pet theory for Toni: people might be conservative rather than outgoing by nature. A case of hardwiring. A yen for familiarity and comfort—two roast ducks on New Year's Day, battered cod every Friday and cheese from *only* Mrs. Finnigan's farm shop. Toni doesn't relish being incompatible with her own child; it's surely to be avoided, at all costs.

What would she do if this best-match guy suddenly wanted to up sticks, emigrate to Australia, like Freddie did? Flamin' Nora! Co-parenting with someone new could be a total disaster. At least Atticus seems steady. Pretty sweet, to be fair. Maybe she could persuade him to co-parent with her. And, more to the point, he doesn't travel too much. He did mention a trip to China when she last slept over, and she feels bad she didn't ask him more.

Her muzziness persists. She drops into her armchair. In a split second, she feels herself ignite. She lifts her right foot; she's tempted to kick over the coffee table. *So* tempted. But no. She lowers her foot. Six fertile years wasted on that tosser Freddie. Why didn't he clear off three years earlier, give her a chance to start over? She curls up, knees to chin, and hugs her legs tight.

Toni admits to herself now—twelve months since the final split— that it wasn't six years she spent with Freddie. Probably four and a half years, if she subtracts their spats and periodic break-ups. They never moved in together.

When he announced his emigration plans, Toni scoured her entire flat for anything he had ever given to her: a designer corkscrew, a travel manicure set—what was he thinking?—all the film books. And a scarf, which she loved. She stripped photographs from their frames—even a group photo taken at Danny's wedding in which she could see only the top of Freddie's head. In her utility room, she found an old gym bag, and she carefully packed all the Freddie-reminders inside as though laying things to rest. It all went up into the small loft. Then she remembered her short stack of theatre programmes; Freddie had snaffled most of them. Sifting through, she weeded out three programmes for productions they'd seen together. Up to the loft, into the gym bag. Finally, she decided the empty picture frames were useless because they carried a memory of the Freddie photos. So they went up to the loft too. There was nothing left. Nothing. And she found the purge surprisingly cathartic. But that feeling didn't last. On the morning Freddie boarded his flight, she experienced a throwback to an old, too-familiar feeling of abandonment. She didn't get out of bed that day. It seemed she couldn't differentiate between a split with a below-par boyfriend and the accidental, life-shattering loss of her mother.

X

Atticus shows his pass at the gate. The security guard hands over a hard hat and reflective jacket, and Atticus strides out onto the site—levelled, apart from one mesa-like mound, some three metres high, at the site's northern end. The mound's slightly angled flat top reminds him of a particular mesa, the Cerro Negro in Argentina—a world away from the dereliction of Dagenham. Until twelve months ago, this site housed a dilapidated and abandoned transport depot, and since then Atticus has supervised the painstaking process of stripping oil and fuel spillages from the soil.

A tracked excavator stutters forward with its bucket raised. The operator stabs the bucket into the remaining mound, scoops and tips soil into the waiting dump truck. Atticus estimates the bucket's volume and quantifies how long it will take to treat this remaining mound of soil. On days such as these, he knows he has the perfect job. As he rocks on his heels, watching the synchronized performance—it's so satisfying to hand over a clean blank canvas—a message pings on his phone. It's from Toni: *Hey, weather forecast good for weekend. Fancy a picnic Sunday?*
Promised to spend the day with Max, my kid brother.
Bring him along?
OK!

X

Toni opens her calendar and makes a new overlay, which she titles "Atticus." A single red dot for each time they dated over the past six

27

weeks, and an extra red dot for the times she stayed over at his place. It takes a few minutes of cross-referencing with messages to pinpoint the sleepovers. She screws up her eyes and sighs. Atticus hasn't met her dad or stepmother, he hasn't seen her flat—no one has stayed over with Toni since Freddie left—yet she's carrying his baby. She opens her eyes and assesses the double red dots—three sets in one particular week, nearly six weeks ago. No problems though. The one time, ages ago, that the condom slipped, she took a morning-after pill.

✕

At midday, Alice's video-call whoops from Toni's screen. Alice is brushing crumbs from around her mouth with her fingertips.

Toni says, "Hey! Alice. Thanks for getting back."

"You're still in pyjamas, Toni. What a life!"

"Yeah. I'm not leaving the flat today."

"Not hung over, then? You looked a bit wobbly after the pub."

Toni rebuffs the comment with an innocent look. "I was tired after a busy day. In fact, I didn't have much to drink."

"Fun night, wasn't it? Look, I've got a student coming in, so I might have to break off."

"I won't keep you. It's not pressing but, um, I've been seeing Atticus for three months or so, and I know he's knocked around in your circle for much longer."

"Danny knows him better but, yeah, I've known him a couple of years." Alice is distracted. Toni assumes she's multitasking.

"It's just, he's kind of quiet, and I haven't made much effort to . . . well, we haven't talked much. Just having fun."

"You want the back story?" says Alice. She makes full eye contact.

"Yep."

"That's only fair. He's been asking around about you."

"Asking who? You?"

28

"I know he's been asking Danny. He wanted to know how long you'd been single."

"So, what do you think of him?" asks Toni.

"He's really nice, actually."

"Nice?"

"Yes. He's really nice."

Toni leans into the screen. "Is *that it*? What about previous girlfriends?"

"I know he had a thing with Bethany whatsit, and that was going well, or so we all thought, but then she broke it off."

Toni screws up her face. "Oh dear. How long ago?"

"A year and a half?" Alice asks herself, looking upwards. "Two years?"

"Was he devastated?"

"He wasn't suicidal, if that's what you mean. Anyway, he seems a steady type. Doesn't talk a lot, but he's not introverted. I guess you know that already. He has a younger brother, lives near his parents. I think he does athletics coaching at his old school."

"I didn't know that." Toni feels deflated—talk about a one-dimensional relationship. "Anyway, he seems to have a good job, construction work."

Alice snorts. "Not actual construction work, Toni. He specializes in land clean-ups. Studied geology—you know, stalactites and stalagmites? He's involved in that new retail project the Chinese are funding out at Dagenham Docks. He's doing the site preparation."

"Oh! I *think* I knew that," says Toni.

"And lovely manners, in case you hadn't noticed." There's a knock at her door. "Hold on. My student's early."

Alice disappears from view. Toni hears her asking the student to wait two minutes. She returns and speaks in a lower voice. "Toni, look, as far as I know, he's uncomplicated. Steady. Better than your last one."

"That's not saying much."

"What's going on? Are things getting . . . ?"
"Not sure. Can't decide if he's my type."

⋈

How is she supposed to concentrate on work? Toni sits at her writing desk and reads the feature she drafted yesterday for *The London Sentinel*. It needs polishing, but Toni closes the document. In her current state of mind, she'll undoubtedly fuck it up, and she can't afford another fail. They spiked her last piece, and she didn't get an apology. It's already a worry for Toni because on the back of being a *Sentinel* correspondent, she wins lucrative public relations work. Toni opens her Costa Rica file. It's all she's fit for: three hundred words on each of fifteen places of interest to visit from Hotel M——, one of twenty-three hotels in the global chain. She's churning out similar crap—well-written crap, of course—for each hotel. It's the kind of commission she doesn't mention to her friends. Her name doesn't appear on the stuff; she insisted on that. In her line of work, reputation is all.

⋈

A picnic without a picnic rug looks shambolic to Toni. Her own tartan rug is rolled and tied with leather straps, and it's slung across her shoulders. She pulls her wheelie cool box through Hyde Park along the path by Lansbury's Lido towards the widest part of the lake. Her pace is unhurried, for she's half an hour early for her rendezvous with Atticus. She rolls her eyes as she surveys a vista of half-arsed picnics, the mess of packaging from carry-out cakes and sandwiches. A crumpled paper tissue blows across her path. Toni believes in cloth napkins.

During the morning, as she prepared the picnic—homemade sandwiches, a lemon cake, real lemonade—she flitted through the videos and podcasts she'd tagged over the past two days. She listened to a roundtable discussion about co-parenting and the threat to the nuclear family, including an interview with Anthony, a music producer, about how co-parenting allowed him to have a child as well as an all-hours career—"I've had zero success in sustaining relationships with women, but I know I'll be a good dad." Plus an interview with Frances, a sustainability consultant—"I don't need a needy male in my life." And a late-night politics show about the possibility, one day, of gestating babies in artificial wombs so that women won't be *burdened* with pregnancy. Could an aborted foetus be revived and transferred to an artificial womb, asks the interviewer? Would the medical staff be obliged to do so? At this, Toni stopped in the midst of buttering bread. An artificial womb? No need to carry a baby? Fancy that! She imagined a conversation with her theoretical Mr. Right co-parent: So, Mr. Right, how would you feel about industrial gestation? Any guy would go for it, she reckons, because he'd be an equal partner, an equal parent, from the start.

As she approaches their rendezvous by the ice-cream stall, she spots Atticus playing Frisbee with Max, his brother. She falters in her stride, thwarted; she'd planned to set up the picnic before they arrived. Atticus sees her, throws the Frisbee in her direction. It arcs away, then swerves towards her, seems to stall. She abandons the cool box, lurches forward, but she's not fast enough. The Frisbee drops and veers again. A final lunge and she's down, flat on the hard ground.

Atticus sprints towards her. He shouts, "You took your eye off it."

"I wasn't ready," she calls back.

He offers his hand and shouts over his shoulder, "Max, run and get the cool box."

She groans. "Knocked the wind out of me."

"Why did you dive?"

"I shouldn't have done."

"Come on. Give me the rug—we'll spread out here."

"I think we'd be better over there, by those trees." She points. "There's a bit of shade."

"Good idea. Hey, are you okay?"

"I'll be all right."

Atticus and Max set up camp by the trees, and in the cool air Toni's nausea begins to subside. She lies down. So far, the afternoon isn't going quite to plan.

"Are you hungry yet, Max?" asks Atticus.

"Not really." Max looks down the slope towards the Serpentine, scanning for potential playmates. He picks up the Frisbee and throws it. Two children, a girl and a boy, break away from their family groups and reach, all hands aloft, as though compelling the Frisbee to fly towards them. Max chases off.

"He's a lot younger than you, Atticus."

He grins. "Yeah. Don't I know it. There's no lazing around at our house, not with Max." He lies on his side, propped on an elbow, and stares at her.

She gazes into his eyes and makes a mental note. Hazel. Her mum's eyes were similar.

"Have you ever been to one of those parties, Toni, that seems perfectly fine and pleasant, and then someone arrives late who totally makes things spark? Yeah? That's how it felt when Max came along."

"That's a lovely way of putting it. That's really sweet, Atticus."

"Everything was fine at home, but then it was better."

Toni looks up. One of those perfect-sky days—wavering Prussian green leaves against an impenetrable cobalt blue. Atticus sits up to watch Max and the other children at play. His shoulders shake as he laughs. He twists around, still smiling. "I'm glad you suggested a picnic. We haven't met up in the daytime before."

"Haven't we? How odd." She changes the subject. "How often do you baby-sit Max?"

"Oh, now and then. I live near my parents, so it's easy to collect him and drop him off. I watch him play football on Saturday mornings. And if I get tickets, I take him to the match."

That's half his weekend spoken for. She bites on her bottom lip.

✳

When they've packed away the remains of their picnic, Atticus shakes out the rug and folds it neatly, but not obsessively so. Toni decides the afternoon has been a success insofar as she's warmed towards Atticus. The feeling appears to be mutual. However, as they walk towards the tube station, she's thrown when he suggests they meet again before his next trip to China.

"China? When are you going?"

"In ten days."

"How long are you going for?"

"Three weeks."

She blurts, "Tomorrow. Come to my place for dinner. I'm going to be crazy busy from Tuesday." She feels sick and sweaty; she has to tell him before he leaves on his trip.

✳

On Sunday night Toni barely sleeps a wink. She sits up in bed as soon as there's a glimmer of light leaking around her window blinds, and she makes two lists.

Atticus Plus:
    Loves children
    Steady job
    Punctual
    Easy-going

Sporty
Travels with his job
Positive outlook
Parents still alive (good genes)
Good-ish looking
Atticus Minus:
Might hate the co-parenting idea
Not a homeowner yet
Might want to move in!
A bit boring?
Football nerd
Travels with his job
Spends A LOT of time with his family
Not serious? Politics?
Not quite handsome

She wishes she'd made this list before the picnic. Some journalist. Anyway, the point of the picnic was not to calculate the sum of pluses and minuses. She wanted to be around him, without the sex. That's all. She can't believe she hasn't worked out his politics. Or is he a fence-sitter? She swings her legs out of the bed, sits with her right palm pressed against her forehead. Stop. Stop. Stop. There's a baby! She shouldn't be worrying about damned politics.

☓

On the dot of six o'clock that evening, Atticus arrives at the seventh floor of Toni's block of flats. He feels elated. A week ago, he sensed she was keeping him at arm's length emotionally—discounting the sex, of course. But with the picnic and then this dinner invite, he feels a wave of relief. As though he's scored a goal after a fallow period. He guesses, from the building's structure and the position of each entrance door along the corridor, that Toni has a one-bedroom flat, possibly two-bedroom. It's certainly bigger than a studio. Before he knocks, he brushes his palm across the door. He nods and makes an approving lower-lip pout; it's not real wood, but it's high-spec. She's invested well.

Toni opens the door, and Atticus can tell from her quick appraisal that he's probably dressed overly smart, and the flowers—a small bunch of white roses—might be a mistake.

She says, "I haven't changed. I spent too long cooking."

He steps over the threshold. "Smells good." She stands back and ushers him along the hallway towards her kitchen-come-workspace. "I like cooking."

"I didn't know that."

He discards the flowers to the steel-topped island where two place settings have been laid.

"Nice space. I like it, Toni. Very workmanlike. Two desks, I see."

"It suits me." She shrugs. "I changed the flat around recently. I used to have my office in the second bedroom, but I found myself working most of the time either at the island or at the dining table. So I moved the desks in here and sold the dining table. I always eat at the breakfast bar anyway. Works great."

"Why two desks?"

"One for doing my writing—the tidy one. The other for admin. But to be honest, I use the admin desk when I'm writing any PR crap. I don't want to contaminate my best desk."

"Two desks, one office chair, and one armchair."

She laughs. "The armchair's for tea breaks. I do have a sofa bed, but that's in the second bedroom now."

"So when friends come over . . . ?"

"I haven't entertained in a long time." She opens the fridge, and with one hand pulls out two bottles by their necks. "Beer?"

"Thanks. I'm planning on getting my own place soon. I'm a bit embarrassed I'm still renting."

"What's been stopping you?" She looks at the bottles of beer, stalls and puts one back in the fridge. She pulls out a cola, levers off the bottle tops, and she and Atticus chink their bottles.

"Other priorities," Atticus says. "I funded some major repairs on my parents' house last year. But I'm getting my own life sorted out now. I'd like to buy a flat this year, then do some travelling."

Eyes wide open. She nudges for more. "Travelling?"

"I've been delaying it. The time wasn't right."

Toni perches herself on a bar stool. Atticus drops into the armchair facing her. "In fact, I wouldn't mind working overseas for a year or two. I fancy a stint in China."

She frowns. "But you travel with work already. Like I do."

"It's not the same as living there, is it? Wouldn't you like to live overseas? Be ideal for a travel writer, wouldn't it?"

"My last boyfriend said the same. He went off to Australia."

"He actually emigrated. That's different."

She straightens her back. "Been doing your homework?"

"Sorry, Danny mentioned it. But, you know, I wouldn't want to leave permanently. I'd go for a year or two."

"Why China?"

"I'm getting to like the place. I visited Qingdao last time. It's like a mini-Shanghai, but with German architecture. I'd love to live there. In fact, I'd jump at the chance if a job came up."

"I went to China with my dad after my mother died." She pauses, shifts awkwardly on the bar stool. "That was . . . nearly twenty years ago." He waits quietly, patiently, for more. She tells Atticus in fits and starts, seems to shrink as she does so—and all the while, she fiddles with a fork, prodding her palm with the prongs—that her mother died in a car accident, her father brought her up. She says that she and her father are close, and she's also close to her father's second wife, Anna, who used to live next door. That is, this Anna was a friend of the family while Toni's mother was alive. Atticus listens without interrupting because he's taken aback that Toni is opening up. He can't understand why it's taken her so long to tell him about her family.

Toni lays the fork down and wipes her eyes.

"You shouldn't bottle this stuff up," he says.

"I don't. I'm always crying."

⋇

The vegetable lasagne is undercooked. Atticus waits for Toni to pass comment, but she seems not to notice. He shovels strategically with his fork, coming at the lasagne from different directions, chopping in, scooping. He takes a last mouthful as Toni puts down her knife and fork, defeated. She's made little impression on her meal.

"I was going to wait 'til later," she says.

"For what?" He takes a swig of beer.

"Listen, Atticus . . ." She pauses. He looks into her eyes—soft brown, they weaken him. "I like you, Atticus, really, but I think we rushed into things. You see, I hadn't had a relationship for over a year when I met you. I'd forgotten how to date and—"

"That's all right." He smiles broadly. "Everything's going fine. We can backtrack and start again. I know it hasn't been romantic, but—"

"No, I think . . . I'd rather have you as a friend. Before we go any further. I can't face a big bust-up like I had with Freddie, and I'm just getting used to being on my own again."

"What?" He can't have heard her right, can he?

"And I need to focus on my work. Things are going pear-shaped; I've had an article spiked."

"Toni! Things are going great. Let's start again—proper dates, like the picnic."

"It's not just that. I'm pregnant."

⋇

She sits in the armchair this time; he sits in her office chair facing her. He has established that she's feeling fine—though he recalls the drinking session last week—and she hasn't seen her doctor as yet. She reckons she's less than two months gone. So, early days.

"Let's get this straight. You *are* going to keep the baby?"

"I haven't decided."

"Am I getting any say in this?"

"I'm telling you, aren't I? I didn't have to. The fact is, I'd already sort of decided—before I ever got pregnant—to sign up for co-parenting."

"What? You don't need to co-parent. You've got a baby. We've got a baby. Why don't we see how it goes? This could—"

"Atticus! We hardly know one another. We're likely to break up sooner or later, and that's traumatic for a kid. If I'm going to keep this baby, it's best to rethink and maybe stay platonic. I think you'd make a good dad."

"You must be fucking joking."

Toni seems to recoil, pushing herself farther back in the armchair. Atticus knows he shouldn't have sworn at her.

He says, "I don't get this. We're getting on really well, and because you're pregnant you want to break it off? Or . . . you're considering an abortion so you can choose a co-parent, a stranger. Have him round to jerk off in the bathroom. Is that how it works?"

"No, it isn't. It's all organized at the clinic, artificial insemination, medical checks and everything." She stabs a finger at him. "And mind your language. This is my *home*."

"Fuck's sake," he mutters, looking away. He takes a deep breath. "Anyway, my genes are as good as anybody's. And do you honestly believe a co-parent would be wholly dependable—wouldn't get distracted, fall in love, want to move?"

"But it's a legal contract."

He leans forward and speaks slowly, quietly. "Have you any idea how hollow that sounds? Are you telling me you'd go to court to make this co-daddy show up on time, stop him emigrating, stop him finding the love of his life, wanting a new family—a proper family! Do you believe it's so uncomplicated? You're being sold a line, Toni."

"I'm not. Lots of people—"

"It's a business opportunity. Someone's exploiting you."

"What? No, no, I don't see it that way. There's so many people wanting—"

"Demand. Supply. That's all it is." He's ready to ignite with pure frustration. His face is burning. Must calm down.

"Please! Don't see it like that, Atticus. You could sign up too, and we could take the co-parent path with this baby. I know you'd make a reliable father, and we can each take time out, catch up on work, have fun."

"Children *are* fun."

He stands. "Never thought *I'd* be a part-time father."

"Well, I have to decide soon."

He grabs his coat, walks down the hallway and stops. After a few moments, he walks back to Toni. "I'll delay my China trip. We're going to spend time together, and we'll sort this out. I want you to keep the baby, and I want to keep seeing you. And, if all goes well, we'd eventually move in—"

"Okay, so what happens? I keep the baby. You're interested for a few months after the baby's born, and then you clear off. I'm telling you, that's the likely scenario. I'll be a single mother with no help."

"Look at me. Do you really think I'm that type?"

"You're a guy! You like the idea of a woman having your baby. But if you decide you don't like me enough, you'll leave. I won't accept the risk, Atticus."

"I wouldn't walk away from the child."

"You don't think so."

Atticus walks over to Toni. She's picking up the dinner plates. "Put those down. We shouldn't be arguing." He leads her across to the armchair, and he sits down, patting his thigh. "Come, sit here." But she perches on the end of the chair's arm and lets her hand hang limp beside him. He takes her hand and caresses each fingertip in turn between his thumb and forefinger.

⋇

Toni wraps four fairy cakes in a fresh tea towel. "Take these for Max."

"So, we'll go to the cinema tomorrow?"

"Yes."

"Can you forget about co-parenting for a while? Park it for now."

"That's not the big decision." She hands the cakes to him, but she won't meet his eyes.

"I know. But honestly? I think we can make it work. We should carry on as we are. And we don't have to move in together if that's bothering you. We can have separate places, have the baby, and still stay over with one another. Just not live together. Then the baby will grow up knowing we don't actually cohabit."

"But what happens when we break up?"

"If we break up, I'll do the co-parent thing with you. But you won't have paperwork with a bloody signature on the end."

Toni pushes back. "I won't be left high and dry. I'd make you sign *something*. And the baby wouldn't take your surname."

He pauses, allows his shoulders to relax. He asks, "Did you consider not telling me?"

"Only for a moment."

"You know, this is a lot for me to take in. You've lived with it for a few days."

"I'd better see my doctor. Find out how many weeks I am."

"Don't make any—"

"I won't. I wouldn't."

BE THE GENTLEMAN

Automatic doors slide open, and Freddie makes his entrance into Blyth's, a downtown Sydney sports bar. The bald, black-shirted barman squints at him as though saying to himself, Is this guy famous?

The large screen on the brick end wall is showing a cricket match. Freddie grins. What a good start. Cricket is civilized, and even better, it's a women's match—pitch perfect for a first date. At some point in the conversation, he'll carelessly mention that he opened the bowling for his university team. This single fact, he feels, establishes his credentials.

He's relieved Australia is playing Sri Lanka. An England Test match would be too tempting; he'd look away from his date. Learned that particular lesson the hard way, a classic dropped catch. He strides across to a booth beyond the bar, which by his reckoning will be less noisy, and drops himself into the leatherette bench so that he faces the bar. His date will enjoy a view of the big screen, which will give her the impression he can take it or leave it when it comes to sport—he isn't a fanatic. From his seat, Freddie can nevertheless watch the match on a smaller screen over the bar.

A waiter, all strut himself, hands Freddie a menu. He orders a pint of Crown Lager.

"Right you are, mate," the waiter says. He pivots on his heel.

The menu is sticky to the touch. Freddie tuts. Could be the harbinger of another disastrous date, so he decides to rehearse his getout. He'll say to Catherine, or Cathy—he can't remember which she prefers—that he's sorry, he bought a ticket weeks ago for a matinée at Eternity Playhouse; he will need to split sooner than he'd like. He'll say he didn't to delay meeting her until next weekend. That's smooth. And she will probably have a get-out herself, and he should allow her time to deliver hers first. Be the gentleman, you fucker.

If his date with Catherine, or Cathy, goes well—that is, if they have lots in common, and that's his main hope this time—then he'll impress her by saying, Forget the matinée! He'd rather spend the afternoon with *her* than sit in a theatre.

Of course, this isn't true. He hasn't bought a theatre ticket. But it could have been true, very easily. It's a regular part of his developing routine. It's how he likes to relax at the weekends. He goes for a morning run, or a walk on the beach, then showers and goes downtown for lunch and a beer. Then the theatre, or cinema, in the afternoon. By going to the matinée, he leaves his evenings free for actual socializing.

He takes a paper napkin and, as best he can, he rubs the greasy smears off the plasticized menu. He hopes Catherine—he'll call her Catherine—is a theatre-goer. With a bit of luck, it's his love of the theatre that actually drew her interest, the real reason she wants to meet. When people put *love theatre* in their profile, it often transpires they only like bloody musicals. He decides he'll clarify the matter this evening by amending his profile. He'll add: *Theatre buff (hates musicals)*.

A woman walks in who could be Catherine. His heart—it frikkin' palpitates! She twists around, looks lost, but then waves to someone at the far end of the bar. He's relieved because he needs a couple of minutes to prepare himself, to remind himself to shake off the professional demeanour.

Freddie, as a dentist, prides himself on his talent for holding one-sided conversations—a professional inevitability. On social occasions, he has to remind himself he can ease off, let other people steer the conversation. By Friday evening, after peering into people's mouths all week, he craves a bit of physical distance—a second professional inevitability, he suspects. Hence his weekend run. Even at the theatre, he sits way back from the stage. Otherwise he finds himself critiquing the actors' dental work. Sadly, that's unavoidable at the cinema—so many damned close-ups.

Eternity Playhouse is one of his favourite venues here in Sydney. Back in London, he booked tickets for most productions at the Donmar Warehouse and the Roundhouse. Toni was a great sport. Even if she'd flown back from a travel assignment and wanted nothing more than a night in with pizza, she'd go along with him. Stuck in his white-box surgery all week, he felt trapped in a white-box flat. Toni used to say, "You book the tickets and I'll come along." She knew he needed an escape. And, without fail, she went halves on the ticket price and after-show dinner.

What he liked about Toni was that she tried her best to keep up, even though theatre wasn't her thing. She talked about the shows afterwards over dinner, remembered the actors' names and what they'd appeared in before, especially if she knew them from the screen. Toni preferred the cinema, which Freddie couldn't comprehend. He tried to convince her that theatre was the higher art form because every performance was a new interpretation, whereas a film was static. The most you could hope for was a director's cut. But she didn't fight her corner. Toni tended to watch films while she was away on assignment. Then, if she'd watched a film she thought Freddie would like, they'd watch it together on the big screen at home.

The waiter comes over, asks if he's ready to order food. Freddie says he'll wait for his friend.

Freddie suggested the sports bar as a meeting place because he knew they could order a light bite instead of settling down to a full meal. There's nothing worse than being committed to a one-hour-plus date when it's obvious there's no spark within ten minutes. He looks down at himself. Are his clothes too casual? Should he tuck in his T-shirt?

He also suggested the sports bar because he doesn't want Catherine to know he's loaded with money. Which he is, by most people's standards. Though he shouldn't rule out the possibility that Catherine is wealthy and might hate sports bars. Has she walked in already, and walked straight back out? He didn't tell her it was an actual sports bar. He told her it was a cool hangout.

Where's she got to? Fifteen minutes late already. Not a good sign. Toni was never late. She always knew exactly where she was going, didn't get lost. Seasoned traveller, he supposes—second nature.

It's a year since he left London. He wonders if it's too late to ask Toni for those other theatre programmes. He likes to keep them in case he goes to a new production. They'll be online most likely, but he prefers the print copies. He imagines that in his dotage—he hasn't shared this with anyone—he'll spend many happy hours thumbing through his programmes and ticket stubs. When he goes home next summer to see his folks, he might drop by Toni's place. He'd love to drop by her dad's. How does that work? Visiting your ex-partner's dad? Freddie had felt special being part of the Munroe family, so arty. Dominic could paint a landscape as perfect as a damned photograph. Freddie couldn't understand why, when Dominic eased off on the private commissions, he'd started painting abstracts—when he had all those skills. Perhaps he was having a crisis.

Toni bought tickets for all the blockbuster exhibitions, but Freddie let her enjoy them on her own. She didn't like him traipsing five yards behind her. She accused him of, what was it? Intellectual laziness. That was it. Forever pushing him away like that.

Freddie reckons that he and Toni could have worked out had she come to Australia. He tried to explain, with a job like his, he had to make changes in his life. Otherwise his years would be lost in repetition. Same surgery, same surgery hours, same commute to work. It's already getting same-y here in Sydney. He could move to a different area of the city every twelve months—create a new journey to work, find the local bars and better routes for his Saturday run.

He checks the time and calls over the waiter. "Bring me some nachos, will you, mate?"

"Sure thing."

Freddie dreads having children. He'd have to settle down—schools and all that. He'd have two decades of the same commute, same everything.

He slaps the table with his menu. Millie could get the programmes for him! She's *his* friend, after all. *He* knew Millie before Toni did. He'll tell her exactly where Toni kept the programmes, second shelf in the living room. Toni probably wouldn't even notice if they disappeared. That's another thing that pissed him off about Toni. *His* friends all became *her* friends. They all seemed to forget that he was their friend first.

That was the spark for their final argument. Toni claimed he *let* his friends drift across to her. She said it was his own stupid fault. He never returned messages; he was lazy. She said his friends all learned that the best way to organize anything social was via her, not him.

Freddie reckons none of the bastards ever mention his name.

A TRAIL OF CRUMBS

September

The car locates a parking space thirty-seven metres from home. Anna Robecchi does not disembark. She has fourteen minutes before the hire period expires, and she ought to give Dominic a little more time with his daughter. She guesses they've had forty-five minutes to talk— assuming Toni arrived on time, which she usually does; Toni says punctuality is a habit she can't break after ten years as a journo.

Since the beginning of Anna's relationship with Dominic, she has ensured, to the point of religious observation, that he spends regular one-on-one time with his daughter. Anna avoids being cast as the intrusive stepmother. Today of all days, Dominic and Toni need time to chat. He's had a week to assimilate the news of her pregnancy. He wasn't shocked as such because Toni had occasionally talked about starting a family. That is, while she and Freddie were still together. And Dominic likes children.

Toni had dropped by without any warning to break the news— she never needed to warn them, they loved her turning up on spec— and she sat with Anna at the kitchen island while Dominic chopped vegetables for dinner. She made no preamble. She delivered the news as simply as she might place a shiny red apple at the centre of the island. "Atticus and I are having a baby."

They couldn't help but fire questions at her: How was she feeling? How many weeks? With a white-knuckle grip on the chopping knife, Dominic asked, "Was it an accident?"

Toni fended him off. "You know I want a family." She didn't linger— said she would let them absorb the news for a few days. Although she addressed the comment to both of them, she looked directly at Dominic.

After Toni left, Dominic put the knife aside and placed his palms flat on the island as though needing support. Anna expected him to cry at that point. It was only natural he'd want Toni's life to follow a more conventional arc. It swiftly transpired that though he *was* upset, it wasn't for the reason Anna expected. He started dissecting the events of the previous few weeks and expressed his opinion to Anna that Toni had stage-managed how to break the news. Anna read his downcast mood—he felt offended, hurt.

Toni had called around—three weeks previously—with the new boyfriend, Atticus. Toni had said, offhand, they were passing by en route to a party in East Dulwich. In his naivety, Dominic admitted to Anna, he had assumed Toni was trying to put his mind at rest; she'd moved on from Freddie and wasn't angry any longer about the years she'd wasted on him. Then, the following weekend, Toni invited them over for dinner at her flat, which she hadn't done for a while. Dominic had clearly taken the invite at face value. He'd thought Toni was out to impress the new boyfriend—to display her close friendship with her father and stepmother. But in light of the news about her pregnancy, Anna watched him brood, even quail, as he realized Toni had been preparing him, *her father*, trying to put him in the best possible frame of mind. He hated it.

Anna had always admired how, up until now, he and Toni had talked plainly to one another. But Anna felt grateful, even warmed, that Toni broke the news to the two of them—surely intentional. Since then, as though a silent pact had been agreed between herself and Toni, she keeps her comments to Dominic to a minimum—sage and conciliatory murmurings. After all, she repeatedly reminds Dominic, Atticus is a sweet, considerate man. He'll make a good father. She also points out that Toni hadn't thrown a teenage hissy fit when Dominic broached their engagement all those years ago. Anna's clincher: "How can a baby be regarded as bad news? Once the baby's born, you'll be the doting grandfather."

This morning over breakfast, Anna said to Dominic as he churned over the sequence of events yet again, "What did you expect Toni to do? Turn up with a man you'd never met before and announce they were having a baby? Obviously, she wanted to break the news gently. It was far better you formed an opinion of Atticus before they dropped the bombshell."

Dominic mulled this over, chopped the top off his boiled egg and said, "Well, no one's died." Given the history of sudden death in the family, Anna felt he'd established a new, unshakeable perspective. Well done, you, Dominic. Without looking up from his breakfast, he asked, "Anna, what do you think her mother would have said?"

The car sounds an alert; the hire period is close to expiration. Anna lifts the bouquet of flowers off the back seat—buying the flowers had been an excuse to leave the house before Toni arrived—and she slides open the door. Dominic probably has no idea that Anna keeps a respectful distance from his relationship with Toni. She never questions any of his decisions in regard to Toni—paying off her university debts, paying a hefty deposit on her flat. Connie would have approved, and it's a portion of Connie's life insurance that he's spending on Toni.

Anna can't claim to miss Toni's mother as much as they do. That would be ridiculous. She misses Connie, but in her own particular way, and she keeps this to herself. It's nearly—she squints as she subtracts the dates—twenty years since the road accident. So it's seventeen years since Anna married Dominic. But Connie doesn't hang over their marriage. Not at all. Anna realizes she's shaking her head, and she smiles. Dear Connie.

Connie would have haunted a second marriage, Anna feels, if Dominic's new wife had no previous connection to the family. Anna, as a neighbour and close friend, was already a part of their lives. So much didn't need to be said. She went to the funeral but stayed in the back pews of the church. And in the aftermath, she cooked the occasional meal, as much as anything to keep a close eye on Toni.

Anna had never thought she'd be a stepmother. It isn't a burden. It suits her fine. Of course, her mother doesn't approve, but then, disapproval is her mother's life's work. A work-in-progress, you might say. She disapproved when Anna turned down a job at Fiat headquarters in Turin, disapproved when Anna left Florence to teach Italian in London, disapproved when she didn't marry in a timely fashion, disapproved when she didn't have children of her own. One day, Anna will do something so outrageous that all her previous transgressions will be nullified, obliterated, forgotten. It will probably take a murder conviction. Or, attempted murder—the prison sentence would be shorter, but the disgrace would be just as devastating. Anna reaches into the bouquet, snaps the stem of a red carnation, and pushes the red flash behind her ear. "Fuck you, Mama," she murmurs. "I'm nearly sixty years old."

She lengthens her stride. Anyway, as the eldest, she escaped with relative ease. Thank God. Her mother had been so preoccupied with Anna's younger brothers and sisters, she didn't stop to consider that Anna would never live in Italy again.

It's a shame Toni doesn't have siblings. As one of five children, she'd have learned while growing up, as Anna had, that parental attention came in short rations. And the corollary, of course, would be equally true. As one of five, she would owe less to her parents. Toni is too anxious over her dad's disappointment. If Toni's prepared to take a risk with Atticus, then that's her decision. It's her life. Dominic needs to understand: it's not about him.

※

Anna finds Dominic and Toni drinking tea in the back garden, sitting on the small bench, silvered with age, that's positioned in the natural suntrap by Dominic's studio. Anna is pleased to see them soaking up the autumn rays. Dominic waves Anna over and calls out, "Toni's been saying this is a great garden for children."

Anna looks around. "Good job we sold my house and not yours." She smiles. "We didn't consider the garden itself, did we? Just the studio."

Toni asks, "Can you fix a swing, Dad, to the bough of the cherry tree? Is it high enough?"

"Should be fine for a toddler's swing."

Toni fetches a garden chair. "You shouldn't be lifting that," says Anna.

"I'm fine. I'm not an invalid. Here, sit down with Dad, and I'll make you a cup of tea. Dad, tell Anna what we've been discussing."

Anna watches as Toni wanders along the curving path, past the raised beds, under the rose-covered arch and past the small water feature—a lion's head set into the boundary wall, spewing water from its mouth into a chipped Belfast sink filled with shells. The shells were brought home from each visit to the coast. Anna tries not to look at the shells when she's in the garden; they remind her that she missed out on Toni's baby years.

"It is a kid's paradise, this," says Dominic. "Toni and her friends used to run around the paths, and we had a sandpit by the studio entrance. Perhaps I should make another one."

They sit facing the sun. Anna tips her head back and closes her eyes. "So, what were you discussing?"

He sighs. "Honestly, Anna, I feel Toni's laying a trail of crumbs. I'm following, picking them up one at a time."

"And the latest crumb?"

"She thinks it might be easier to spend a few years overseas—somewhere they could afford childcare, and somewhere interesting for her work. The thing she's worried about is losing ground with her career." He leans towards Anna, though there's no one to overhear him. "Between you and me, the way I read this . . . I don't think she's prepared to depend on Atticus long-term."

"How do you feel about them going overseas?"

"Bad. But then, I never considered *my* parents' opinions."

"Is it Toni's idea to go abroad? Atticus might be driving it."

"She seems pretty keen. She can work anywhere as a freelancer, but she might need a pseudonym—work permits might be a problem."

Anna is still soaking up the sun, eyes shut. "Where, though?"

"She's not saying. Not yet anyway. She'll probably throw me another crumb next week."

"Smart girl." Anna laughs softly.

"At least she didn't have a baby with Freddie. Never really liked him."

"Neither did I."

He nudges her arm with his elbow. "Well, you never said anything."

She opens her eyes. "It wasn't my place to comment."

X

Toni returns carrying a tray with Anna's tea and a plate of buttered fruit loaf. "I'm starving."

"You're not eating for two yet," says Anna.

"I don't have morning sickness like Millie. Just hungry all the time."

"And these travel plans," says Anna. "Would you wait until after the baby's born? Or go abroad beforehand and come back for the birth?"

"Nothing's definite yet." She devours half a slice of the fruit loaf and pipes up, "You know, with both of you having more time on your hands, this could be a fantastic opportunity. You could both visit us."

⋇

Dominic clears the table after dinner. He says, "It's a shame Toni couldn't stay for the evening."

Anna tried to persuade Toni to stay, but Atticus had already invited her over for a family dinner. As Toni made to leave, she said she needed some advice. "Atticus hasn't told his parents about the baby. I've met them a couple of times. What do you think? Should we tell them together, or should he tell them on his own?"

Dominic grimaced and looked to Anna.

"He should tell his family on his own," said Anna. "We stayed calm when you told us, but if his mother or father react badly, if they say anything harsh, it's best you're not there to hear it. You can never unhear it, and that wouldn't be a good start, would it?"

Toni nodded. Anna looked across at Dominic and opened her eyes wide, encouraging him to speak. Dominic stepped forward, hugged Toni and said, "Once the baby's born, everyone will be fine. Try not to stress. Your mum used to say that babies need happy vibes." Toni pulled him close.

With the table cleared and the kitchen tidied, Anna asks Dominic if he's planning to go back to the studio.

"For an hour or so. I want to look through some reference books this evening. I'm going to copy a Mary Cassatt drawing for Toni. As a gift."

"Wouldn't she like a more personal painting—one of your own abstracts?"

"I think she'd appreciate a picture for the nursery. *A Goodnight Hug*, if you know it." Anna pouts and shakes her head.

"It's more understated than Cassatt's usual thing. It's an embrace, but doesn't show the mother's or the child's face. Anyway, I'll do another trawl. I like *The Boating Party* too."

"I'll come over later and take a look."

✕

Anna pulls out a photograph album from the oak chest that serves as a coffee table in the living room. She flips through the pages and finds a spread of photos showing Toni as a child with Connie. She wonders if Dominic should paint one of these. Or is this the wrong time for sad reminders? She leafs through several more pages until she finds her favourite shot of Connie. It's underexposed, taken around the time Dominic was away in South America on one of his commissions. He was gone for over a month. A couple of evenings a week, Anna came round to keep Connie company. Toni would be tucked up in bed, and Connie would sit in the wicker armchair, exactly as she is in this photograph. Connie wasn't a big drinker. But on one particular evening, one drink became three drinks, and Connie began talking about her youth, how she was dumped by the first love of her life. At the time, Anna was incredulous. She couldn't imagine anyone ever dumping Connie.

Anna angles the photo album to avoid the reflected glare of the wall lights. As she studies Connie's face, she relives the dread realization when they first met, that if she *let* herself, she'd fall in love, even though Connie was evidently straight, married.

She'd felt crushes in the past for women, but that's all they were, crushes. Kind of pathetic. Shutting the album, Anna wonders if she started the affair with Dominic as a way of keeping Connie close.

✕

At ten o'clock, Anna takes the open bottle of wine and two glasses over to the studio. They often do this at the end of an evening. It's something *they* do, that Dominic didn't do with Connie. Anna smiles as she walks along the garden path. Her mother had warned her against moving into Dominic's house. She'd already committed to the move, but for once, she took heed of her mother's concerns. Anna insisted, and Dominic agreed, that they should swap around the bedrooms and buy a new marital bed. The rest of her efforts were more subtle. At the outset of their relationship, Anna had felt she had to create new routines so that Dominic would feel—from daybreak until his evening's end—that life had taken a different shape, different from his first marriage. Connie was slow in the morning. So Anna made an effort to rise early. She still takes a tray of tea and toast to the bedroom every morning of the week.

And just as Anna created a new start to Dominic's day, she made a change to Dominic's routine of working in his garden studio after dinner. Connie had regarded his studio as a private lair and rarely ventured in. She took him tea occasionally, didn't linger. So Anna takes wine and stays to chat. She loves the smell of his studio. She loves Dominic, and she loves the idea of him too. The artist in his studio. He calls it his shed, but she refuses to follow this lead—it's his right to be self-deprecating, not hers.

As she tiptoes across the now-damp grass of the back garden, she recalls the one time she offered to clean up the shelves, wipe down the tins, clean the windows. He said, "What? Clean my space?" She didn't offer again.

Standing outside the studio, she smells the pine cladding. She taps on the door with the bottle and steps inside—she inhales. This is the moment she adores.

"Have you chosen?" she asks.

"I think so. Take a look."

Anna pulls over a chair, *her* chair. Dominic decided, soon after they were married, that if she insisted on coming over every evening, she'd need somewhere to sit.

Dominic flicks back and forth between the two pictures reproduced in a monograph. He says, "Personally, I think Toni would prefer *The Boating Party*. It's not so sentimental. And, see, there's a small child in the boat."

"If they *do* go overseas, it might be a nice gesture, kind of appropriate. Sails billowing and so on. And the colours are so muted, lovely."

"Fairly loose brushwork. Fun to paint."

Anna pours the wine. They chink their glasses.

"Connie would love it too," says Anna.

FAVOURITE AUNTIE, FAVOURITE UNCLE

November

Woke this morning, performed my usual routine while waiting for my little sis, Millie, to finish in the bathroom. Lay flat on my back with my hands splayed on the bedsheet, kept my eyes closed, imagined blood pumping through my arteries, flowing back through my veins.

I'm trying to work out exactly how I went wrong today.

Lying there, I said to myself, as I always do, It's Just A Body. Gets me from point A to point B. The question I then asked was the same question I've asked myself every morning for the past decade: Do I want to reach point B as a man or as a woman?

I'm not even sure how I make the call. It's either a synapse-y thing or it's a purely physical impulse. Anyway, I don't like to overanalyse the process. This morning, I struggled to decide, so I adopted a second strategy. I spread my legs, tried to decide if I did so in a male way or a female way. That may seem ridiculous; even I recognize it's funny. Anyway, I still couldn't decide. However, strategy number three seemed conclusive; when I sat up and swung my legs out of the bed, the move-ment felt feminine. Sat on the edge of my bed, closed my eyes again, didn't feel male, not in that particular moment.

Looking back, I recall murmuring "Snooze" when the alarm sounded. Pretty sure I did the same ten minutes later when the alarm sounded again. The point is, it takes me a little longer to dress as a guy, to get the contour garments right, to flatten out my breasts and thicken out my waist. Perhaps, deep down, I wanted to save a couple minutes.

So my current embarrassment has been precipitated, it's fair to say, by no one other than myself. Should have it down to a fine art by now. I'm weary of getting it wrong.

I stride along London's South Bank on this perfect balmy evening, a man in drag. My attire: scoop-neck black jacket over dove-grey T-shirt; knee-length straight skirt in powder pink over matching pink straight-cut trousers. Picked from the left-hand side of the wardrobe rather than the right.

I knew I'd made a bad call during our late-morning meeting with internal audit. These are never pleasant encounters, all about pinching pennies, saving time, at the expense of quality and the small mat-ter of job satisfaction, which doesn't feature in month-end accounts. Unfortunately, my colleagues and I were inconsistent. We vacillated between measured responses and out-and-out annoyance. Well, I snapped. Said we already spent too much of the day on our time data. I'd have said the same whether I'd turned up as female or male. But I detected my male self coming to the fore; my voice rose from deeper.

Hate it when this happens. Wish I'd slicked back my hair. And I'm mortified by my accessories; I should chuck this croc-effect grab bag in the Thames. Stick to the black leather backpack from now on—can't go wrong with that. I want to walk with my hands pushed down in deep pockets, wear thick-soled, heavy flat shoes with fat laces, walk with my toes pointing slightly outwards and let my shoulders roll. I settle for a slight swagger. Oh sod it! I'll walk how I want.

X

I don't head straight to the underground. I stop at the terrace bar of the British Film Institute, take a table tucked away in a corner, under a space heater, and sit facing away from the other customers. A waiter with close-cropped hair takes my order for a large glass of red wine. I smile at her, tell her I need the washrooms. She points them out and says she'll place a reservation notice on my table.

I slip away to the washrooms, stare into the mirror and blush under my makeup. I slick back my hair with water—what a relief that is—and wash my face. From the neck up at least, I feel more comfortable. The androgynous thing isn't for me, but I can see the advantages. I smirk at my reflection; children are still starving around the world while I stress over my stupid skirt and handbag. I take a deep breath and return to the terrace as the waiter arrives with my drink.

I read for a while—can't go home just yet or Millie will realize something's amiss. She's expecting me home much later, around ten o'clock, after my voluntary session on the helpline. What a stinking day all round—internal audit, wrong clothes and then, worst of all, I get sacked from a voluntary job. Un-bloody-believable. Millie would probably laugh, and I couldn't blame her if she did, but I won't let on. I'll tell her I'm stopping my Tuesday volunteering because she's so close to her due date. I'll say it's Sod's law that she'll go into labour when I'm mid phone-in. She'll be pleased I'm taking my responsibility so seriously: I'm my sister's one and only birthing partner.

I send her a message: *Hope to leave early tonight. All okay?*

Millie replies: *All quiet. Don't rush xx.*

Losing the volunteer job is more than merely embarrassing. It's created a hole in my CV. I'd hoped to add my volunteer boss as a personal referee. Just goes to show—most do-gooders are pretty staid, or at least that's the evidence from this evening's session.

Things came unstuck during my second phone-in, when I helped a woman see her love triangle in a whole new light—revisionism, I like to think, is my speciality. I suggested to my caller—let's call her Phoebe—that if she looked at her love situation in a different way, she didn't have a problem at all. She went silent at that point, so I knew I had her full attention.

Phoebe had discovered her boyfriend—let's call him Liam—had fallen in love with a guy he met through work—let's call him Steve. But Liam didn't want to split with either Phoebe or Steve. He loved them both; he didn't feel he could devote himself to just *one* person. I suggested to Phoebe that her boyfriend wasn't lying. I asked her to try to imagine that for a moment. After all, I know from experience it *is* possible to love more than one person at a time. I told Phoebe that if she accepted this premise, she could come to an arrangement with Liam. They could still see one another as long-term partners, but from time to time they could indulge one another, allow each other to follow their romantic impulses.

Phoebe went quiet again. She thanked me and ended the call.

Half an hour after this phone call, my supervisor—let's call him Dez—hollers over to me from his cubicle. "Robyn, in here, if you please."

Dez, who must be all of twenty-three years of age, gave me the raised eyebrow, didn't even ask me to sit down. He told me not to come back next week. He then added, in a lowered voice—presumably to save embarrassing me within the open office—"Don't come back anytime." He'd monitored my conversation with Phoebe and informed me that my unconventional advice had been inappropriate. Phoebe—"the client" as Dez referred to her—had actually phoned back to complain. I hate charity workers who adopt corporate-speak. They're not fucking clients; they're *callers*, they're desperate people.

Dez told me I hadn't followed protocols. Protocols, my arse. Clients, my arse. I told him, in language he might understand, that he was "behind the curve, by two decades." His petit bourgeois attitudes, I told him, should be fucking archived.

X

I order a second large glass of wine and a plate of bruschetta. I try not to drink at home these days; it's not fair to Millie. Still get a thrill ordering a *large* glass. I can afford one now. This year I'm solvent for the first time in my adult life—I've avoided asking my parents for help. My modest savings will now cover a decent two-week holiday. And I've upgraded all my ageing tech. Not only that, I've thrown away my threadbare threads, and back in January, I bought my first proper winter coat; the first I've bought since leaving home—*almost* can't wait for serious winter weather. And moving in with Millie means I've said goodbye to damp flats and sleeping on friends' sofas in return for spring cleaning. Word had got around I was pretty shit-hot on the domestics.

I know what it's like to live on next to nothing—believed I had real experience to offer the helpline. I actually loved my work there, if you can call it work. Prior to the Phoebe incident, I helped plenty of people to analyse their problems, isolate the issues and prioritize their actions. I helped people with real problems who couldn't afford private counselling, who were too terrified to step inside a lawyer's office—terrified of the cost.

So here I am: a qualified lawyer, solvent and trying to give back to society. Well, society will have to get along without me for a while. I'll focus on Millie and my own circle.

X

The door to our ground-floor flat opens with a bang against a tall box. I squeeze myself into the hallway. Millie, in her pyjamas, is carrying a steaming mug from the kitchen and says, "It's the cot."

"Jeez, it's enormous."

"You should have messaged on your way home, Robyn. I'd have made a drink for you."

I follow her through to the living room, which is lit by a reading lamp and the flicker from the imitation wood burner. Light dances across the embossed spines of the books on our alcove shelves—leatherbound books passed down to me and Millie by our late grandfather. He'd thinned out his collection in retirement, kept the books that deserved reading more than once in a lifetime. He told us he'd leave them to us because he knew we'd read them. And Millie's attempting to read the full shelf of Russian authors before the baby's born.

"How's progress?" I ask nodding at the book by the armchair.

"Finished the Yevgeny Zamyatin novel. Starting the first of three by Lyudmila Ulitskaya."

Millie eases herself down into the armchair, rests the mug on her swollen belly and looks up. She frowns at my slicked hair. "Wardrobe fail?" She smiles in sympathy.

"Got it wrong again." I roll my eyes. I don't elaborate, and Millie evidently takes the hint.

She says, "Good news, Robyn. I heard from Toni. Her first article from Shanghai will appear online tomorrow. Can't wait to read it."

I drop into the sofa. "It's a shame she won't be here when you give birth."

"I've been thinking today . . . I know I said you could be godmother." My hand automatically goes to my forehead. "Sorry! You're still the godmother. Don't worry. But would you mind being *joint* godmother with Toni?"

"That's all right!" Total relief. "Why would I mind? Go for it. And Aiden's still going to be godfather?"

Millie winces, as a child anticipates a reprimand. "I've changed my mind."

"Ouch, Millie. Are you sure?"

"I've been messaging him. He won't give me any indication of *how long* he'll be gone. He might never come back, you know."

"He'll be a lifelong beach bum. Is that what you think?"

"I'm feeling more and more pissed off with him. I've had to do all this on my own. Sperm banks. Fertility clinics. I'll have "father unknown" on the birth certificate. If Aiden had *stepped forward*, everything would be a million times easier. I mean, it could have happened by accident." She sips her drink.

"Well, it didn't, Millie." I give her a look that says, Get over it.

"It's his mother, Betty, I feel for. If this baby were Aiden's, she'd have a new lease of life. She's desperate for a grandchild."

I feel drained, and I sigh heavier than I intended. "I need to get changed."

"I'm sorry, Robyn, you look tired. I'll make you a drink."

"Don't be daft." But Millie is already pushing herself out of the armchair. I step forward, take both her arms and help her up. We laugh. Millie, always the dainty one. She's a bus now.

※

I settle into the sofa. I'm wearing my checked pyjama shorts, a clashing striped T-shirt, and I've pushed my hair up into a beanie hat. "Obviously, I'll be favourite auntie even if I'm only a joint godmother," I suggest. And as soon as the words are out of my mouth, I feel weird because I realize I want to be favourite uncle too.

"Don't be so sure. Toni is pretty competitive," says Millie.

"But when's she coming back?"

"Eight weeks before she's due. But they might go back to China for a couple of years. There's a project in the offing for Atticus."

"That's all right, then. I'll be fully bonded by the time she's back for good. I'll be reading all the bedtime stories."

"Talking of bedtimes . . ." She looks from the corner of her eyes at me. Sheepish. "Mum and Dad are coming over on Saturday. They're going to set up the cot."

"I'd have done that." Shit. It's going to hang over me all week. Mum and Dad can't bear to see me in men's clothes. For them, and them alone, I plan ahead for an androgynous look. Millie has actually overheard Mum saying to her friends, "Robyn fashions herself on those catwalk models with their little-boy looks."

"I *told* them you'd help me, but you know what they're like. Dad insisted."

"What should I do about Hunter?"

"I thought that was off. Thought you'd argued," says Millie.

"It's on again. He'll be here from tomorrow evening. Can we put them off to Saturday afternoon?"

"If I suggest that, they'll guess you've got someone staying over."

"Well, that's their problem."

Millie cocks her head to say, Don't be so hard on them. I don't know why she's become so conciliatory; does pregnancy sweeten you? Our parents are hardly euphoric she's going solo, and they're far from happy we're living together—because of my *lifestyle*, as they call it. When they offered to help Millie buy a flat, Millie had wanted to apply for a joint mortgage based on both our salaries, but Mum and Dad wouldn't go along with the plan. They blustered over totally baseless concerns, mainly arguing that I might take a job elsewhere and need to buy my own place; the implication was twofold—they wanted to help with the deposit for the property, but more pertinently, they didn't accept that Millie and I would be living together for the long term. So Millie has decided, unbeknownst to them, that once the baby is born and Mum and Dad are busy bragging about their grandson, she'll start the paperwork to add my name to the mortgage, and she'll write a will making me the executor and legal guardian for the baby.

"You know what I find weird?" says Millie. "There's Toni, two months ago, in a complete flap because she's pregnant—I mean, almost a meltdown—and everything's working out perfectly. Her dad seems absolutely fine about it. Her stepmother is preparing a nursery in the family home. Painting fluffy clouds and cherry blossom trees across the entire wall; Toni sent me the photos. You should see it. It's incredible. And Atticus, bless him—he's one in a billion—he's all loved up over Toni and the baby. How does Toni land on her feet like that?"

"That's the Munroes for you. Uncritical by nature, I guess. Anyway, we'll make a happy home for *our* baby." We both laugh. We're in the habit of saying "our baby." I've even adopted the royal *we* when I talk about Millie. "We'll breast-feed." That caused hilarity in the pub last week. But Millie and I have talked everything through. We always have done. We know everything about one another, so there's no chance we'll ever have a serious fallout. Millie's still hopeful of finding a partner, but next time she won't take a chance as she did on Aiden. He said he could handle her disinterest in sex, but to my mind he realized he'd made a mistake. Millie's main worry, and it's understandable, is that even if *I* end up with a long-term partner, it won't ever be exclusive. She's worried about men and women breezing through the baby's life, the child's life, the teenager's life. What if one of them—what did she say—was an *inappropriate* adult? Strewth! I couldn't imagine that. But the more people we had in transit through our home, she said, the greater the risk we ran—it might not be fair to the child.

So this is the deal: I won't bring any one-night stands back to the flat. Not that I'm into that. And if I have a partner who isn't known by anyone else in our friendship circle, then I've to keep them away from Millie and the child until I've known them for at least three months. No parties at our place unless Mum and Dad take the baby for the night. No smoking indoors. Millie *alone* is allowed to arrange baby-sitters. Finally, I'll take one week's holiday each year to give Millie the chance to get away on her own. Then, Millie says, we can say "our baby."

TONI CAN'T GET ENOUGH OF CHINA

December

"I'm going to write about Chinese egg and chips this week," says Toni.

"That's a good one," says Atticus.

Though it's a cold day, it's as dusty as ever. They pick their way along broken pavements in an area beyond the commercial centre of Shanghai. They're catching a lunch break together, heading to a small eatery that Atticus regards as a special find. He's braver than he used to be—at one time he'd have dismissed the Xinjiang Food Heaven. It looks a dive, and most of the customers seem to be students or low-paid office workers. His colleague, Cheng, brought him to the restaurant when Atticus transferred from the London to the Shanghai office two months ago—a temporary transfer, yet the office agreed to cover Toni's flights.

Cheng taught Atticus the Mandarin for "not too spicy." Since then, he has dined at the Xinjiang Food Heaven twice a week, and each time the young waiter greets him with a broad smile and the same question, "More chilli, today?" It's a Uyghur restaurant, run by a family from the far west province of Xinjiang, on the old Spice Road to Europe. The Uyghurs are the pasta specialists of the East. As Atticus recalls his last lunch there—laghman noodles with lamb sauce and peppers—his mouth waters and, simultaneously, his stomach rumbles.

Atticus carries Toni's handbag because that's the norm in China. Seeing his reflection in a shop window, he grins—it's a lopsided grin. It's funny how he's melded with local customs; his shock threshold is much higher, and he reckons that's a good thing. He and Toni pass the egg sellers who stack their stalls with hundreds, if not thousands, of eggs. They're stacked so high that a stranger to the area might fail to notice, behind the egg sellers, two squat onion stalls positioned by the entrance to an alleyway. Atticus ventured down that alleyway with Cheng some weeks ago, discovering a food market that sweeps like a tsunami along the many dark back alleys off the main street.

Cheng was a patient guide. He pointed out the specialities as well as everyday foodstuffs and fast foods: potsticker dumplings fried in large pans of oil; xiao long bao—a chicken-stock soup with dumplings filled with pork; black sesame bao and red bean bao—breakfast snacks, so sweet and sticky they made Atticus gag; stall after stall of fresh noodles; a stall juicing pomegranates; yet more displays of eggs—the smallest being pigeon eggs; and a wet fish market with long lines of blue plastic baskets filled with crab and eel. Atticus committed Cheng's commentary to memory, regurgitating all the facts and anecdotes to Toni later that same day. He felt he'd discovered his nose for news because Toni immediately followed up with her own visit to the market and found a bunch of story leads. Already she's written a short feature about the strange juxtaposition of the xiao long bao chef and his market neighbour, a chiropodist, whose pitch is just large enough for two wooden stools—one for herself and one for her customer.

Thanks to that feature, Toni now has her own weekly column in *The London Sentinel*. Atticus feels the title, China Tales, is a tad uninspiring, but Toni had long dreamed of securing a regular column, and she dismissed his quibble about the title: "It's a huge step forward for me. If the content is good, the sharing could be stratospheric." Toni can't get enough of China.

They reach Xinjiang Food Heaven with its cracked plastic signage and steamed-up windows. It's hemmed in by a cycle repair shop and a cigarette kiosk. As they step inside, they're engulfed by the smell of cumin. They're early enough to nab their favourite of the six tables—the one closest to the small galley kitchen. Toni takes a seat facing the galley's open doorway. Atticus knows she'll take mental notes. He twists around and sees the same three family members standing at their usual stations—mother and father and the father's brother, crammed elbow to elbow in front of three steaming vats on a blackened gas stove. He turns back and watches Toni's eyes as she inspects the kitchen interior, and wonders if he'll be reading about the restaurant in her next column for the *Sentinel*. He hopes so because he's curious to see which details Toni picks up on; he's invariably surprised. Yet he attempts to match her; it's a game he plays on the sly. He notices that the benches and stools are mismatched—battered but more or less clean. And the restaurant feels crowded with only four other diners, each sitting alone.

Toni refocuses on Atticus. "My next column is sorted out. The egg-and-chips photos are absolutely brilliant. They're perfect for China Tales. And it's a double whammy—there's a high hit-rate when travel combines with food."

She took the photos at the Wangfujing night market on the first evening of their recent trip to Beijing. At the time, Atticus had had one thought: how to fill his stomach as quickly as possible after their train journey from Shanghai. But Toni? Well, without fail, she has her antennae up for a story.

"That street market was the best part of the whole weekend," he says.

"I can't wait to go back."

He says, eyebrows raised, "If we're going back to Beijing, we shouldn't delay the trip too long. You're pretty big already."

"I'm bigger than Millie at twenty-four weeks." She places her palms on either side of her baby bump, takes a deep breath and puffs out her cheeks. Atticus laughs.

"Hey, the photo you've chosen for the article—the egg-and-chips piece—you don't mean the photo of me trying to eat the fried egg?"

"Tempting, but no. It's the one showing the bundles of long chips—like bundles of twigs—with a fried egg slapped on top of each bundle. The way they're all carefully stacked, raking back . . . it looks gorgeous. Totally improbable, but gorgeous. It's such a crazy riff on the British greasy-spoon café."

"I tell you what. I'm going to Shenzhen in two weeks' time. I can take a trip out to that artists' village, Dafen. If you give me the best photo, I'll ask one of the painters to make two copies."

Toni crinkles her nose. "Sounds a bit naff."

"No, listen. I'm serious. The artist could send the finished canvases to us by post, and I'll get them stretched and framed here in Shanghai. We can have a painting each, copied from the same photo. Or I can give the artist two slightly different photos, different angles."

"Atticus! People think we're weird already, living in separate flats in the same block. There's no way we're having identical fucking décor."

"Don't swear, Toni." He mock frowns. "Baby might hear. And, by the way, I think I've decided on a boy's name. On . . ." He pauses. Toni is wide-eyed. "Marco. So, Connie for a girl, naturally. And I'd like Marco for a boy—goes well with Atticus."

Toni reaches across, takes hold of his hand. "Good choice. I can live with Marco."

The proprietor's son, a teenager wearing shorts and a T-shirt, sidles up, "More chilli?" He laughs. Atticus shakes his head, points at the photos in the plasticized menu, ordering black tea and cardamom to start them off, then for himself, the Uyghur dish of polu—rice pilau with lamb and lamb fat, carrots and dried fruit. Toni points at spiced soup with tiny meatballs, and a small naan with chopped chives. The boy whirls around, shouts the order across the kitchen.

Toni says, "Anyway, what about your morning? Finished that proposal yet?"

He shakes his head. "So frustrating. I'm waiting for data from one of the directors—keeps promising. Then the London and Hong Kong offices are keeping me waiting for updated bios. And I don't like the proposal's introduction."

"I thought you used software for writing abstracts."

"Only when I'm desperate. The results are always turgid."

The face she pulls says, you poor thing. "It should be easy enough, really. It's an interesting project—Asia's biggest clean-up."

"Nothing sounds sexy with soil remediation in the title. I've rewritten the opening paragraph about six times this morning."

"Cut to the chase, Atticus. Skim through the document and look for a phrase or a sentence that snags your interest. Pretend you're writing for a general reader. Everyone loves an anecdote. Or find a great statistic."

He dips his head and looks up at her as if to say, It's easy for you. "Anyway, I've a dozen other problems to sort out, and the deadline's pressing—"

"Relax, will you?" She splays out her hands on the table. Atticus can see there's a pep talk coming. "When I write a travel feature, I always start in the middle of the action. At the moment of highest drama." She pauses, then repeats, "Highest drama."

"I'm not sure that's applicable."

The teenager brings out their orders—the plates and bowls are as mismatched as the restaurant's furniture—and sets them down with the calculated delicacy you'd expect in a five-star restaurant. The boy's dedication stabs Atticus in the heart.

"Atticus, just chill out. In my work, you see, I'm a flâneur. I try to take in the big picture by absorbing all the small details. Basically, I try to capture the essential, um, unfamiliarity of any given situation." Atticus isn't convinced this is going to help. "Or, lift a great quote from someone in the industry."

He knows it's good advice. Anything presentational is her forte—he saw it in the way she handled the news of her pregnancy. She slipped into crisis management mode. Not that public relations is her thing, exactly, but she studied the theory during her journalism studies. In a crisis, she told him, the correct way to handle bad news was as follows: total honesty, with information released in bite-sized chunks, in as short a time frame as possible. Ideally, the worst news should be released first, but sometimes you have to hold back. She said, "When the time comes to tell your parents, don't simply blurt out that I'm pregnant. I don't think they'll cope with a blunt statement."

Atticus doesn't like such window dressing. Makes him feel dishonest. His parents, *he* decided, could take it all in at once. They'd rarely been critical, and they were grateful to him for renovating the house. As it turned out, he'd expected too much, and now there's an edge to all his conversations with his parents. They've lost their easiness with one another, and he hopes the baby's arrival will patch things up.

"Look, I'll give you a hand with the intro this evening," she says. "This is the big one, isn't it?"

"Yeah. We're saying the project will take three years, not two and a half. You still feel okay about that?"

"Are you kidding? China's a gold mine for me. I only need to walk outside; there's a story on every block. Have you noticed the elderly woman with her sewing machine? She sits by the roundabout at the end of our street? She has an old wooden chair, and her machine sits on a folding metal table. You must have seen her; she's there every day, wearing a thick coat with a high collar." He looks blank and shakes his head. "Anyway, I spoke with her this morning. Well, I didn't speak. I explained in international sign language." She laughs. "I showed her my bump and explained I needed some clothes let out. It won't cost much, hardly anything, and I'll get another month's wear out of everything. It's a great piece for the column: there's me with my best work clothes, purchased from a chichi boutique in London—well, I can exaggerate a little—handing them over to an old woman sat on a pavement in Shanghai. And no receipt."

He puts his hand to his mouth and gasps. "Chilli!" At the sight of Atticus, the teenage waiter doubles over with laughter, and his mother comes out of the kitchen to steal a glance. While Atticus blows in and out, Toni's phone vibrates. She picks it up.

"Message from Millie!" she says, evidently surprised. Millie doesn't have time for idle messaging; the baby is only two weeks old.

Atticus takes a slug of water. "Anything wrong?"

"Says: 'All's well. Rudy's thriving. I'm knackered. Just to let you know, in case you want to send a message, that Aiden's mother—Betty, you remember?—she died at the weekend. In her sleep. I won't get to the funeral. Don't think I could handle it. Love Millie, kiss kiss kiss.'"

"Couldn't handle it? You mean, with a newborn baby?" says Atticus.

Toni pushes her shoulders back, trying to stretch. "No, it's not only that. She won't want to see Aiden—he'll have to fly back from wherever *the hell* he is now."

"She's still mad at him? Because he wouldn't father the baby?" Atticus attempts to cool down his mouth, taking sips of water and fanning his mouth with his hand.

"There's more to it than that." Toni's eyes are watering. Atticus wonders if he's missed the point.

She looks aside, lost in thought. He follows her gaze and guesses she's staring at the bowl of steaming hot soup, which the young waiter sets down heavily in front of an elderly diner. A dirty crack runs down the side of the bowl from a large chip on the rim. Crikey, if the bowl breaks right now—

Toni stares back at Atticus. She says, "It's like this: Millie knew how much Betty wanted a grandchild. So Millie must be thinking, you know, *what if.* Imagine, Atticus. If Aiden had agreed to father the baby, then Betty would have seen her grandchild before she died."

Atticus hands Toni his thin paper napkin. She dabs her eyes, blows her nose. "It's harsh, I know"—her voice cracks—"but I hope Aiden feels a total shit."

PART TWO

2084–2085

PART TWO

THE ADOPTION

March

Don't say bottle babies, Rudy Dack tells himself, though he fears the slang is already imprinted.

His wife, Simone, sits in the control seat as always. The car veers into the grounds of the clinic and scrunches along the gravel drive, making Rudy feel anxious on Simone's account. They sweep through a forested perimeter and emerge to see a glass block of a building.

Simone turns to him and beams. "It's modern."

"That's a good start, isn't it?"

"The gravel drive . . . I was worried."

Rudy knows the gravel drive conjures images of old buildings for Simone. She dislikes old brickwork and iron railings. Smooth red bricks in particular drag her down. It's not that her childhood was dire; her parents were not deliberately neglectful. Yet when she'd left home for her university studies, she couldn't bring herself to return, not even for a brief visit. She left it all behind—her family and their suburban home with its smooth red bricks and black gloss railings. Rudy is the only person who knows about Simone's architectural distastes. He admires her love of all things new. She always faces forward.

✕

"We're due to birth a baby in an hour," says Dr. Kristina Christophe. "So I'll need to break off shortly to meet the parents. Let's take a tour of the wards now. I've booked a table for you in our guest restaurant; you can enjoy a leisurely lunch, on my account, while I'm overseeing the birth."

They follow Dr. Christophe across the atrium in the direction of the gestation wards.

"There's no point going to the first ward. There isn't much to see there. The foetus you're looking at today is in the third-trimester ward."

Rudy cringes. He loathes the word *foetus*—the cold heartlessness of the word—with its intimation that an ungendered *it* hasn't as yet earned its passage.

"Can we see the second-trimester ward too?" asks Simone.

"Okay. And I'll also show you the control room. Then, after lunch, when you've had time to take it all in, we'll talk through the family details and your obligations should you decide to go ahead. How does that sound?"

"Just fine."

"Perfect," says Rudy. He squeezes Simone's hand as they walk with Dr. Christophe along an evenly lit, glass-walled corridor. The large glass panels are coloured in five shades of creamy yellow. Rudy feels he's walking through a dream.

"So we'll skip this one," she says, pointing at the first-trimester ward.

"Are there any adoptions at this stage of gestation?" asks Rudy. In an ideal world, he'd like to start the bonding process earlier. He wants to be sure that his bond with the child will be as strong as Simone's, and the sooner he starts the better. He suspects that women might be quicker at making the emotional attachment. Though he doesn't agree that women have more innate caring skills, a notion that seems to persist, annoyingly so.

"If a foetus were orphaned at this early stage we'd delay offering it for adoption. You see, if there's going to be an emergency in this clinic, it's going to be in there. Once the embryonic period is complete, and when most of the foetal body surface responds to touch, we transfer it to the second-trimester ward. We aren't rigid, though; if development is lagging slightly at twelve weeks, we keep the foetus in the first ward a little longer." She smiles. "It's not a production line."

After a second's silence, Dr. Christophe laughs lightly.

"What's the . . . failure rate?" asks Rudy. Simone pulls a face at him, but he refuses her rebuke.

"Well, the rate is coming down. The figures are in the public domain. Close to single figures now—eight per cent, give or take."

As if on cue, red lights set into the corridor floor begin to flash. There's no audible alarm. Two female medics emerge from a side corridor ahead of them. Dr. Christophe, Simone and Rudy stand aside as they rush past. Side by side the two medics shoulder through the double doors of the first-trimester ward.

"Don't be alarmed. It's not necessarily an emergency," says Dr. Christophe.

They enter an elevator and Dr. Christophe requests the viewing gallery. The lights dim as they ascend. They step out into an even more dimly lit corridor. Dr. Christophe gestures towards windows that run the entire length. It takes a few seconds for their eyes to adjust.

"I thought the baby wards would be brightly lit," says Simone.

"That's only in the marketing material. We don't want the images to look too sombre. In reality, as it's dark in a mother's womb, we try to create similar conditions without having a total blackout. We all prefer to see the foetuses—the medical staff and the parents."

Rudy and Simone gaze down into the second-trimester ward. Though at first sight the ward appears to be a tangle of tubes and pulsing monitors, it soon becomes clear that the tangles are set out in a repeating pattern along the length of the ward, in three rows. In the midst of each tangle sits a tear-shaped bottle that reflects the green data on its overhead monitor.

"So much equipment. And it's so quiet," says Rudy.

"Well, it would be," says Simone.

Dr. Christophe smiles. "It seems quiet to us, but it's noisier for the foetuses. We record the mothers' and fathers' voices and feed the sound into the foetus flasks during gestation. We follow a natural daily rhythm—no voices during the night, just the sound of a parental heartbeat."

"Do you switch off the voices if the baby is orphaned?" asks Simone.

"We haven't had many cases—a handful in five years—so there's no fixed protocol. I try to dissuade the adopting parents from deleting the source-parent voices. We have concerns over continuity."

"You mean the foetus might miss the parents?"

"Not exactly. We feel some aspects of brain development might falter."

"Oh dear! We don't want to risk that," says Simone.

"In the case of the foetus you are considering today, the parent is a solo mother. I'd recommend keeping the mother's voice and adding both of yours."

Dr. Christophe walks ahead, and they follow her along the viewing corridor. With his eyes fixed on the glass bottles, Rudy feels he is watching a time-lapse. The sizes of the foetuses increase as Rudy and Simone follow the lineup. They come to a halt near the end of the ward. Directly below them, one male foetus is hugging himself.

Rudy has been careful not to give Simone the impression that a boy is his preference. He accepts that a girl would bring equal joy, but he suspects he'd prefer messing about with a son. But then, he knows he's being romantic. There's no guarantee he'd replicate his friendship with Aiden, his godfather. Not that Aiden was physically affectionate. His visits were sporadic. Rudy's closeness to him arose through shared pleasures—tough hikes during which they barely spoke. And they both kept goldfish. Rudy knows that even a biological son might be very different from him. With an adopted child, it would definitely be a matter of chance. He tries to push these thoughts aside as he scours the glass bottles, but he can't. Boy, boy, boy, girl, girl, not clear, boy, girl.

In their marriage classes, Simone had opened up more than he'd expected. She said that if they were going to have a family, she didn't want a son who was biologically related to her. More than one child was also a no-go. Rudy accepted her conditions. It was a compromise he made willingly because he felt sure Simone offered him a true lifelong marriage. He saw himself as a devoted one-woman man; he didn't wish a repeat of his own upbringing with his mother and his Aunt Robyn, or Uncle Robyn depending on daily, it seemed, shifts in the zeitgeist. Rudy gave up keeping track of the men and women transiting through Robyn's chaotic love life. And his mother, Millie—well, she eventually gave up on finding a fella, only to embark on an erratic succession of girl crushes, which in the main were crushingly unrequited. For both the women in his childhood, their love interests were, ultimately, disposable. Drove him to fucking distraction.

So he's going along with Simone's wishes: a non-bio, one-child agreement, which negates her anxieties over sibling rivalry.

Sibling rivalry—that's how he and Simone refer to it, though they don't talk about it so often. She was bullied at home. It might have seemed like low-grade stuff—pushing and shoving. Hair tousling that was deliberately heavy-handed—fingertips squeezing her skull. So painful. And relentless teasing. In any case, her parents didn't protect her. Just the once, when her mother walked into Simone's bedroom and found her daughter pinned to the floor by her oldest brother, his hands around her neck. Her mother dragged him off and pulled him down the stairs. But he wasn't grounded. Simone, at heart, felt let down by her mother. Why hadn't she been more protective?

So Rudy and Simone agreed on adoption. Rudy finds it odd that as adopting parents, they can in theory choose the sex of their child. Yet if he and Simone wanted a biological child, he'd be viewed as insensitive should he admit he'd rather have a boy.

"And next," says the doctor, "the control room, which monitors each artificial womb, around the clock, checking nutrient levels, oxygen feed, waste removal and so on. It's safer than a natural pregnancy once the fertilized egg has bonded with the womb lining."

The control room, in its essentials, looks no different to the monitoring and diagnostic centre for any production process. Dr. Christophe waves down to her colleague, and she in turn acknowledges the visitors.

"I'd love to meet the technicians down there, Dr. Christophe," says Simone.

"I remember now. You're both engineers. I'm sure we could arrange a technical tour if you go ahead with the adoption."

"I reckon my current job is pretty similar to your control room operation," says Simone. "I'm in remote problem-solving, diagnostics—for engines, not babies, of course. But mistakes can be equally catastrophic. What about you, Rudy? Would you like a tour?"

"I'm more interested in the first-trimester operation." He turns to Dr. Christophe. "I'd like to see the wombs as they arrive from the manufacturer, and see how you connect them into your bio-support system. And I'd like to see how you introduce a fertilized embryo. If I ever switched from aeronautics to biomechanics, I'd be the guy at the end of the manufacturing line checking each baby . . . sorry, each foetus flask. Or I'd be part of the setting-up operation in the first-trimester ward."

"Takes a calm person for that kind of work, doesn't it, Rudy?" says Simone. She places her hand on his back.

He and Simone met at work, and he often muses that the odds were stacked against them as a couple, work-wise: he performs the final quality checks, while she diagnoses faults in operation. Fertile ground for sideswipes. It seems to Rudy that Simone was attracted to his calm, steady nature. No sharp edges; that's how she sums him up. Totally laid-back.

In the third-trimester ward, the foetuses look robust. It's now evident to Rudy that the younger foetuses in the previous ward have more wriggle room.

"I don't know why people call them bottle babies. The vessels are not solid," says Dr. Christophe. "They distort if the foetus is moving. Parents are so thrilled if they visit during their baby's active time. They can place their palms on the vessel. They can see and feel the baby moving."

"Is the orphan baby here? Can we see it?" says Simone.

"Yes." She lifts her index finger, waves it back and forth, and stabs. "There he is—middle row, fifth from the left."

ЖС

"What do you think, Simone?" says Rudy. "Can you imagine taking him home?"

The French windows of the visitor restaurant are folded open to welcome the first warm day of spring, and Rudy and Simone sit overlooking the clinic gardens. There's a skittering noise outside. They catch sight of two squirrels making a helter-skelter descent of a thick-trunked and peeling eucalyptus tree. Simone laughs and says, "It would be lovely to have a big garden like this."

"So? You've not answered my question."

"Yes. I can imagine taking him home. I can imagine playing with him in a garden like this. I mean, what's the point in having a garden if you don't have children? And we've no other children in our lives."

Rudy has long accepted this thick gloss over the truth. Simone has three nephews and two nieces—the children of her three brothers—but she chooses to have no contact. "There's no halfway house," she told Rudy early in their relationship. She explained that all those years—the constant jibes, the physical bullying—left her nothing to build on. She told him more than once that she had never understood if they hated her because she was a girl or if they hated having a young kid around.

Rudy always tells her, "Everyone deserves a fresh start." He knows she takes consolation from the remark; she responds by hugging him.

"We're agreed, are we?" says Rudy.

"We'll tell Dr. Christophe we're good to go."

⋊⋉

After lunch, they meet Dr. Christophe in her consulting room, which has one window overlooking the second-trimester ward. There's a blind, fully open. Rudy wonders what might prompt Dr. Christophe to close it. Etched plaques are arranged on the wall behind her as though crowning her head: a General Medical Council certificate, plus a certificate for a doctorate in biomechanics from the University of Tokyo, and a photograph of Dr. Christophe holding a baby. Two grinning women stand on either side of her.

"Who's in the photograph, Dr. Christophe?" asks Rudy.

"Ah yes. My first delivery of a child with no biological father. They were set on having a daughter, so the baby was conceived by parthenogenesis—using two eggs; one, less mature than the other, acts as a pseudo sperm. It's interesting you should notice the photo, because we're dealing with a similar case with this orphan, insofar as there's no father. There never was a father, I mean. The mother was a solo parent who conceived with synthetic Y chromosome—my third such patient—and she didn't mind if the baby was a boy or a girl."

"Does solo conception make any difference to the adoption?" he asks.

"In one aspect. Before we accept a solo parent for remote gesta-tion, we require the name of a next of kin; someone who is willing to sign a legal document which states that he, or she, has the financial resources to take responsibility for the baby if the parent dies during the gestation process. We need to ensure that if the solo parent dies, either accidentally or through illness, we're not faced with a legal issue at the time of delivery. Of course, the risk of maternal death is higher when the mother opts for remote gestation. They live a little more recklessly, go skiing and so on."

Simone jumps in: "How did this particular mother die?"

"I can't tell you specifics at this stage, but if it puts your mind at ease, it was an accident. In fact, a bicycle accident."

"So who *is* the next of kin?" she asks.

"I'm coming to that. It's her brother, her only sibling. But *he* has fallen ill and can't fulfil the contract. Our lawyers decided to release him from responsibility. And as a consequence, we have this unusual situation. It's fortunate we still have people like you who are willing to adopt."

Rudy shuffles in his chair. "Will the brother want access to the baby?"

"I definitely recommend that you offer plenty of access. You can offer access in a variety of forms. Face-to-face contact can be negotiated down to one visit per year near the child's birthday. But this brother is very ill, so I'd encourage you to be generous in this regard. He has lost his sister and now he's alone. They'd planned to raise the baby together."

"How sad." Rudy turns to his wife. "What do you think, Simone?"

"It seems so tragic and . . ."

"Yes?" says Dr. Christophe.

"Well, you know. We'll be drawn into all that sadness. I didn't expect this complication. I assumed the baby had two parents and they'd both died and there were no relatives. Rudy?"

"We should perhaps meet the brother before we decide. Can we do that, Dr. Christophe?"

"You would have to meet him before we progressed. He has the power of veto. He might decide to give up the baby for enhanced state adoption, with all the educational privileges afforded to clinic orphans—our insurance policies are comprehensive."

"It's less than straightforward, then? We thought we'd crossed the main hurdle with our own profiling," says Rudy.

"You're right. That was the major hurdle. It allowed us to recommend you as suitable adoptive parents." Dr. Christophe pauses before pressing on, since Rudy and Simone have run out of questions. "You should have a quiet chat together. Why don't you take another look at the gestation wards? Come back here in, say, twenty minutes."

They leave Dr. Christophe's consulting room and head back to the viewing gallery. They hold hands as they look down into the third-trimester ward at the orphan boy. He appears to be frozen.

"It's a pity he's so still." Simone pouts her disappointment.

)(

Rudy and Simone take their usual weekend constitutional to Holland Park, which they prefer to Hyde Park and Kensington Palace Gardens because it's off the tourist trail. Over recent weeks, they've nudged the baby into a routine, bringing an order of sorts to their own lives. Routine and cosiness go hand in hand. They pick up their usual croissants and coffees from the deli on Holland Park Avenue and push their pram—the latest model—up the sweeping road to the park entrance. There's a steep path through woodland. Rudy sees a magpie and a squirrel fighting, or playing—he can't tell which—then they emerge onto a vast lawn that slopes down to the West London Opera House. Rudy has already recognized two families from their previous weekday visits.

"Here, or the Kyoto Garden?" says Rudy.

"Here, I think. We can stretch out for ten minutes before feed time."

They set up camp, spread out their tartan picnic rug and lie on their backs, their faces to the sun.

"When Julia starts kindergarten, Rudy, we'll get to know a lot of local families. We'll be able to meet them here and let the kids play together."

"By then we won't be so bleary-eyed."

She rolls over and inspects his face. "Hmm, you do look a bit tired."

"You slept through it all last night."

"You'll be glad to get back to work, won't you?" she says.

"Not really. If anything, I'm worried I'll be less focused on the job. You know, thinking about Julia." He turns onto his side to face Simone. "I sometimes wonder if I'd feel the same way with an adopted baby. I'm sure—"

"Oh, Rudy, I kick myself now. We should never have started that process. They didn't make it easy, did they? Obligations to the brother . . . Aren't you relieved?"

"What do you think?" He kisses Simone on her forehead.

"We couldn't possibly be any happier. That's what I think," she says.

Rudy rolls onto his back and smooths his palm across the picnic rug. He recalls how he and Simone explained their change of heart to Dr. Christophe. They returned to her office from the viewing gallery and told her the arrangements were too complicated. They didn't want to meet the brother. Dr. Christophe sighed, but recomposed herself. She fixed a smile on her face and said she understood their misgivings.

He'd looked up at Dr. Christophe's photograph on the wall. How many years would it be, he asked, before men in this country could become solo fathers?

"I've just received approval to do my first. The first in the UK as a matter of fact. The clinic has recently gained accreditation for the procedure. We'll create an egg from the father's stem cells. But, I thought you wanted to adopt?"

Simone spilled the beans about her childhood; she admitted she wanted to have a child who was biologically unrelated to herself—or, more to the point, unrelated to her brothers. She said, "Rudy, I'd rather have a baby that's genetically all yours than have a baby that's genetically unrelated to either of us. I'm sure you'd prefer that too."

Dr. Christophe agreed to start the paperwork for solo parentage and made a provisional booking in the gestation suite.

As they stood to leave, Dr. Christophe said, "The adoption idea wasn't motivated by altruism, was it? If you'd explained your family background, Simone, I might have suggested this course of action in the first place."

With his fingertips, Rudy rubs the wool fibres of the picnic rug. He hears the loud thud of a football being kicked hard. In his mind's eye, the ball flies in a high arc across the wide expanse of grass. And he tries to imagine himself, a few years from now, kicking a football around Holland Park with Julia.

As happens so often when he muses on Julia growing up, his thoughts slip back to the dimly lit viewing gallery. He imagines the orphaned foetus, *the boy*, moving within the baby bottle. He imagines the boy turning, pushing out his elbow, causing the womb to distend. He believes that he and Simone would have made a different decision had the boy moved.

But he didn't.

THE COLOURS SHOULDN'T
WORK, BUT THEY DO

June 2085

It's the first-morning rite for Dr. Kristina Christophe's holiday. She sits up in bed with the hardback notebook and sharpened pencil which—as soon as she unpacked yesterday—she placed on the bedside table. In readiness. She studies the handwritten lists within. It's not an easy decision. She closes the notebook and lightly brushes her fingers across the exquisite marbled-paper covering. The rich colours mingle so naturally that the artist's hand at work is unimaginable. Blobs of warm green—a scattering, it seems, of random-sized pebbles along a river bed—separated by rivulets of burgundy red and overlain by mostly smaller blobs of gold and sky blue. The colours shouldn't work well together, Kristina muses once again, but somehow they absolutely do.

She bought the notebook, on impulse, and at nauseating expense, during her honeymoon in Venice. It had been one of five such note-books in a sparse, understated window display—quality and longevity seemed to be guaranteed. More than a mere notebook—an objet. And because of the cost, the notebook was the sole memento she took home.

Their honeymoon in Venice delivered all the romance that Kristina had craved during a chaotic courtship. However, in the years subsequent to the honeymoon, she came to realize that she'd been deluded; Edward had no romance. The city itself had been her romantic partner. Or rather, romance had been conjured not by any murmured words or deft gestures—that hadn't been Edward's way—but by the sublime contrast of young love set against a backdrop of architectural decay.

Although she and Edward separated two years ago, she has kept her memento. She gathered other reminders of her failed marriage in a box, which sits on the high shelf in her walk-in wardrobe alongside lesser hauntings—fabric she's failed to make into cushion covers, boxes of shoes purchased in haste and worn once. Kristina has kept the notebook because over the years, sixteen in total, she has listed on its narrow-lined pages all the books she read during her married life, and the books she would like to read in her singleton future. She associates the notebook less with her honeymoon and more with the transient but true pleasure of a good read.

Choosing a book from these lists will set the tone for her holiday. After ten minutes' deliberation, she underlines *"A Room with a View" by E. M. Forster*—she prefers to start by rereading a classic—and places a pencil tick by the five titles she'd like to read by the end of her two-week break. When she finishes each novel, she'll strike through the title in her notebook and add an asterisk if she feels it's worthy of a reread. These asterisks give her a warm feeling. She hasn't listed her books in any digital community: the notebook is the closest she'll ever get to owning a physical library. She feels she has left it too late in life to start collecting print books. There had been an opportunity when her mother was downsizing and offered Kristina her book collection. But Kristina had been living in a small flat, so passed on the offer. How she regrets that decision. Even if the books weren't her cup of tea, they'd have made a fabulous display.

At home, she keeps the notebook propped up on the mantelpiece. Whenever she hears of a good romance, she adds the title in pencil to one of the lists:

Romance in the classics
Romance in historical novels
Romance in contemporary novels
Romance in speculative fiction
Romance in gothic fiction
Romance in biographical fiction
Romance in prize shortlists
Romance in comedic fiction
Romance in short stories

A southerly breeze carries the sound of waves lapping on the shore. It brings to mind one of her favourite quotes, and she flicks through the notebook to find her notes on Harriet Prescott Spofford. *The winds were warm about us, the whole earth seemed the wealthier for our love.*

She closes the notebook, inspects the pools of gold and blue on the front cover. The colours remain as fresh as the day she bought it, but then, she takes great care to avoid any scuffing. When she travels on holiday, she wraps it in a nightdress. Since her separation, she has bought a new nightdress for each holiday—Edward would never have noticed if she'd done so during their marriage.

When she and Edward met as hospital trainees, they hit it off straight away. They shared a similar sense of humour, similar taste in music and games—though not books—and the sex was good because it felt urgent; they had so little free time together. So following an eighteen-month courtship—though *courtship* suggests a romantic strategy that simply wasn't there—they decided to marry at the end of their training. They didn't get around to buying an engagement ring; Kristina didn't push the idea because she thought at the time, foolishly so, that an engagement ring might be a token of gender subservience.

Nevertheless, she stage-managed several almost-romantic moments amid their busy hospital schedules. These were rarely intimate dinners à deux because they also struggled to keep in touch with friends. Kristina became adept at organizing picnics, and when she and Edward bought their first house, she organized barbecues. She didn't mind being the social secretary in their relationship; she was the natural organizer between the two of them. And Edward's working hours were more chaotic because he specialized in accident and emergency.

Kristina strokes the leather spine of the notebook. It's funny. Edward loved the drama of A&E, but he never showed any interest in reading thrillers, nor any fiction. On the rare occasion he asked what book she was reading, she'd say, "I'm catching up on the shortlists," or "Historical fiction, medieval," or some such—she never mentioned romance. She had decided in her late twenties that as a medic, she read quite enough serious material. The pressure was constant—to read this journal, that journal, the other journal. The way she came to see it, her professional life was dedicated to the betterment of others, so her spare time ought to be her own. And she could meet the pressures of her day job, in the long term, if she learned to find peace in her time off. Ever since, she has carved out time for pleasurable, unputdownable reading. She asks herself when she reads a book blurb: Is this a good book for a Friday evening after a long week at the clinic? If in doubt, she confers with Elizabeth.

Elizabeth is an online buddy who is Scottish but lives in Texas. That's all Kristina knows about her. Kristina suspects, reading between the lines, that Elizabeth is a grossly underemployed public administrator—someone who looks busy but is in fact spending her office hours reading fiction. Elizabeth is a prodigious reader of romance, and the administrator for a romance readers' forum. On the face of it, she and

Elizabeth have nothing in common other than their appetite for a romantic quest.

✕

Kristina slides open the door leading from her bedroom to the deep terracotta terrace that runs the length of the villa. She shields her eyes against sunlight reflected off the Mediterranean and Ligurian Seas. From the terrace, perched high above the yachting marina of Menton, the last town in France before the Italian border, Kristina feels the rush—the French Riviera stretching into the distance, so clear today: the high-rise apartments above Monte-Carlo and the succession of headlands—Roquebrune-Cap-Martin, Cap-d'Ail, Saint-Jean-Cap-Ferrat, Juan-les-Pins. She mentally pinpoints her favourite coves, her favourite headland restaurants. She's unsure, but she believes she can make out the offshore solar farms near the Îles de Lérins. This is her fifth holiday in this villa—the second time without Edward—and she'd never stay anywhere else on the Riviera. It occurs to her that if she ever wrote a novel herself, her opening chapter should describe this panorama, exactly as it is now: an immense sky with individual fluffy clouds—as a child might draw—and the sea, brought to life by discrete patches of diamond brightness scattered as far as the horizon, amid dark malevolence. It strikes Kristina as a metaphor for . . . life itself! She huffs. What does she know about writing novels?

She wishes that *just once* Edward had said during their holidays here, "You'd love this book. You *must* read it." Back in the early years of their marriage, she'd felt confident that she and Edward had enough in common. They were mutually respectful, being professional equals. A sound footing, you'd assume. But she began to wonder—as early as their fifth wedding anniversary—how they were going to fill the years, and she doesn't doubt that a similar thought occurred to him. Holidays were the worst. They'd find an idyllic restaurant in the Italian countryside, or

93

overlooking the sea, but it would soon become obvious that neither she nor Edward had any interest in what the other had to say. She became embarrassed when they resorted to chatting about medical matters, the world of work.

Her birthday was a downer, every time. Edward seemed loath to buy her a birthday present. He'd remark on how lucky they were to have such good jobs. He'd say, "We don't need to buy presents; we can buy ourselves whatever we want, when we want it." Undeterred, Kristina kept a secret pinboard to remind herself of anything Edward mentioned that suggested an ideal present. On *his* birthday, he'd remark, "What a good memory you have." It didn't cross his mind to make more effort himself.

They don't have children—they'd consistently shied away from that decision—though perhaps they made a mistake there.

Maybe true opposites fare better. Kristina keeps her eye on a small fishing vessel as it weaves its way through the moored yachts and splutters off towards the Italian coastline. Since she moved into remote gestation at the clinic, she has edged ever closer to this conclusion. The unlikeliest couples seem perfectly happy. Yet those *seemingly* well matched can be riven with unexpected complexities.

Take Rudy and Simone, a handsome couple who came to her clinic just over a year ago. Kristina has no doubt they'd have created the most beautiful baby, with minimal intervention. But they denied themselves that possibility because—and she didn't put this in her notes—they were messed up. As Kristina saw it, they had everything going for them—similar professional jobs, each clearly in love with the other, no complications in their medical histories—but, sadly, their individual neuroses bore down on this major decision in their lives: Simone wanted a child *only* if it was disconnected from her genome. For some reason that Kristina can't quite fathom, Rudy willingly accommodated Simone's wishes. So Kristina agreed that Rudy could become a solo father, and the result was a healthy baby girl. Simone became a stepmother of sorts to Rudy's child.

Kristina shakes her head. So many shades of fucked up, and she has seen so many of them. Her current theory—which she wishes she'd come up with sixteen years ago—is that two people are well matched when their individual neuroses are complementary. In her own case, she knows she's needy because her parents were emotionally disconnected from her. And Edward was unable to make physical expressions of affection because, she guesses, his parents, although loving, became hypercritical in their drive to see him succeed.

She makes her first cup of coffee of the day and returns to the terrace with her reader and notebook. Sitting astride the low terrace wall, she makes a plan of attack for her holiday. Today, she'll take the train from Menton-Garavan along the coast to visit her favourite haunts in Nice. She'll hang out in cafés, read a book, sunbathe on the beach. She opens her reader, cross-checks with her notebook and pulls up the novels on her reading list. She opens each novel in turn and reads the last page. It's a bad habit—even Elizabeth disapproves—but she hates the disappointment of an unhappy ending.

※

Later that morning, at Menton-Garavan station, Kristina buys a return ticket to Nice. She plans to head straight to the restaurant on Rue Lascaris, which serves the best shellfish platter on the Riviera. She takes a seat on the platform, looks up at the monitor—train due in sixteen minutes. It's tempting to start her first holiday read—E. M. Forster's classic—but the station is too bleak, feels inappropriate. Better to save that book for the beach this afternoon. Instead she opens the final chapter of *Miranda Mostly*; she might as well finish it before the train arrives. She skims across the paragraphs—it's an easy read—but as she reaches 98 per cent, with the train due in three minutes, she finds herself captivated; *Miranda Mostly* concludes with one of those authorial flash-forwards that Kristina *utterly adores*. She reads the final sentence as the train pulls in. She steps aboard knowing that although Miranda and Gregory have married against their families' wishes, they will win everyone around as soon as their first child is born.

)(

An hour later, Kristina will arrive in Nice, and much to her disappointment, she'll find there's no table free at the restaurant in Rue Lascaris. Deflated, she'll walk down to the quay in Old Town and discover that a one-time shabby art deco café has been renovated and reopened as a brasserie, evidently popular. She'll take the only free outdoor table; she'll assume that the man at the next table is French or Italian, which will suit her because she dislikes making small talk with other tourists. Twenty minutes later—Kristina's shellfish platter having been served— he'll remark, in English with a Scottish accent, that she has ordered well. He'll tell her that he's taking a day off from his work as a perfumer, and he'll visit suppliers in Grasse the next day. "How interesting," Kristina will say. He'll offer to take her along: "It's a lovely drive, and I'd love some company. You could look around Grasse while I have my meeting, and then we could have lunch. I know all the restaurants." But she'll turn him down.

Were she to accept his offer, Kristina and this man with no name would begin a love affair. They'd spend a blissfully happy year together in London despite their lives being so different—professionally speaking, that is—one being of such consequence, the other seemingly frivolous. But during a cold snap one day in early spring, he would slip on ice and die from head injuries after several weeks on life support. Inconsolable, Kristina would return to the Riviera and swim out to sea until she could swim no farther. She would slip below the waves and make no effort to save herself.

If the man did not slip on the ice, Kristina would realize over the following year that she and this man were, in fact, profoundly incompatible, and their relationship would dissolve in acrimony.

Instead, having rebuffed the perfumer's offer, Kristina will pay the bill for her shellfish platter and quarter carafe of Vouvray. Normally, she would order an espresso, but she'll want to escape before the perfumer strikes up conversation again. She'll walk down to the long pebbled beach, and after reading *A Room with a View* for half an hour—to allow her lunch to settle—she'll strip to her bathing costume and take a swim in the near-still waters of the Mediterranean. She has always adored swimming in the sea. She'll swim out of her depth, then float on her back and look up at an unblemished blue sky. She'll say to herself: This will be a perfect holiday.

DREAMS BEFORE THE START OF TIME

Untitled No. 97, 1992, Dominic Munroe

A photograph. A small open tin of paint sits on a cobbled path close to a wall. The cobbles are black, granite most likely; the paint is pure baby blue; the wall is stippled with grey render. A makeshift stirrer stands in the paint. But the stirrer is longer than necessary—it's a strip of timber moulding—no doubt conveniently at hand rather than fit for purpose. And the top end of this stirring stick leans against the wall for support. There's a double danger of imbalance: If the top of the stirrer slips sideways, it will tip the tin over. Or a passerby, distracted, could knock the whole arrangement across the cobbles.

X

The skylight is a black rectangle. Marco Munroe sits in his office at the top of the house, tucked under the eaves. Free of disturbance—for his daughter is asleep—he looks through his grandfather's photographs.

They came to light only after his death. Now Marco imagines his grandfather lying on the pavement to photograph the tin of paint. *That's* dedication. Marco frowns as he swipes through the images, admires Dominic's tenacity in recording everyday street scenes in a body of work built up over sixty years. It's more than dedicated; it's *doggedness*. And Dominic kept it secret, never exhibiting the images, nor attempting to sell them as far as anyone knows. A secret project, Marco wonders, or simply private?

In his student days, Marco was tempted by photography as a career—that is, commercial rather than fine art photography—but opted instead for industrial design. It's crazy, to his mind, that Dominic didn't upload this collection, or at least the best of the collection, to a stock photo library. He wonders if he should do so himself, provide an income stream for the family. It's a fantastic resource—over three thousand images shot between 1990 and 2050. On average the collection contains one photograph per week for Dominic's adult life. So did he take a weekly stroll specifically to find a good shot, or did he carry a camera at all times, constantly alert?

Marco suspects—in fact he has persuaded himself—that his grandfather stuck with this photography project for one overriding reason: namely, to protect his own sanity, to maintain his own sense of balance in the world. Sure, he made a good living copying the old masters, but he needed to satisfy a deeper impulse. Marco reckons his grandfather shot the photographs—these are not "snaps"—as a reminder to himself, as a statement: *This* is me. *This* is Dominic Munroe.

In this reimagining of Dominic's past, Marco reveals his own starry-eyed tendency—one he accepts as a recurring flaw. He had believed everything was going well between Colin and himself. But Colin moved out; Marco never saw it coming.

〤

Untitled No. 633, 2002, Dominic Munroe

A close-up of a keyhole with a polished brass escutcheon, in a red exterior door. A sprig of rosemary protrudes from the key hole. Marco imagines an art deco stained-glass window, circular, set into the door, out of shot. The sprig of rosemary is surely a message: I called but no one was home. A signal from a family member or good friend, someone who is close to the house owner but has no key—a cousin, a nephew, an aunt. One image but several plausible stories. Is it safe to assume that no one was home? Or did the owner hide behind a curtain, having checked who'd rung the bell? Did the visitor drop by with good news, bad news, or gossip? Did the owner return home and, on seeing the sprig, feel frustrated or relieved?

There must have been a rosemary plant in the front garden. Again, it's out of sight. And it must be well established—you wouldn't tear a sprig from a small specimen.

Marco smells the rosemary.

He admires Dominic's brazenness; he'd spotted the keyhole, walked along the path—maybe four or five paces—through the front garden of a stranger's home, and shot the photograph. That's how Marco sees it. Ah, but . . . Was Dominic the visitor? Of course, *he* put the sprig in the lock. That must be it, mustn't it? In which case, are these photographs a form of diary? There's no need for words when a photograph recalls an entire episode.

It occurs to Marco that he should take a leaf, or a sprig—he grins at his own joke—out of Dominic's book; he should pursue a creative interest for no particular purpose. Definitely visual. He isn't a wordsmith like his mum, definitely closer in his interests to Atticus. (Marco never did call Atticus *Dad*. He can't remember a time when his parents were anything other than Mum and Atticus.) He needs a sustained spare-time activity, a hinterland. For it's the hinterland that completes a person.

✕

Untitled No. 2262, 2034, Dominic Munroe

A photograph of a kid's drawing on a weathered brick wall. At the base of the wall, on the pavement, there's a small pile of coloured chalks. The line drawing on the brickwork—in red, yellow, white and blue—depicts a woman in a big hat walking a dog with a big tail. Marco enlarges the photograph, looks in close-up at the woman's cartoon lips. Stuck between her lips is a crooked cigarette butt, a real one, and there's another cigarette butt jutting from the dog's mouth.

Marco barks a laugh. He imagines the scene: the child artist found the butts on the pavement, or in the gutter, and picked them up. Without any plan in mind, the kid screwed them into holes in the brickwork—bored kids *do* that kind of thing—and only *then* did the kid draw the woman and dog around the cigarette-butt interventions.

For now, Marco won't hatch any plans for Dominic's photographs. He'll simply enjoy swiping through them—after all, he's getting a new angle on his grandfather—though Marco admits the photographs aren't exactly avant-garde; there's no shock of the new here. Dominic's intention was perfectly simple. By shooting these photographs, he trained his eye; the act of observing made him ever more observant.

Marco closes Dominic's collection. He opens another file. It's a video of Amelie, one he watches most evenings. It's a ritual that stops him ruminating over his sporadic-at-best love life.

In this clip, Amelie is seven months. She hugs herself in her artificial womb, thousands of miles away in a private clinic in Mumbai—highly rated for solo conceptions for men, and evidently operating below the radar of regulators. Marco had never warmed to the idea of using donor eggs. Going solo felt right, and no one outside his close family needed to know. He planned ahead, took a job in Mumbai, and returned to England at the end of his contract with a baby, his own baby.

There she is with her dimples, still the same. Is she *smiling*? Or full of wind? There's no knowing. Or is she dreaming? He prefers to think so. A dream before the start of time, her time here in the world.

Amelie appears at the door, hair unkempt. "I heard you laughing." She steps in, and the projection of her foetal self distorts across the folds of her nightdress and across her face. Marco turns off the video.

"Oh dear. Didn't mean to wake you."

"I wasn't even asleep. You should let me stay up later, Dad."

"Come over here, then. Look at this funny photo—one of Grandad Dominic's."

He pulls up the image. Amelie gazes, smiles vacantly—she's more tired than she'll admit. Then Marco enlarges the dog's head. She bursts into laughter.

"I wish you'd known Dominic," says Marco.

"I *do* know him!"

"Not really. Not for real."

✕

Marco returns to Dominic's photographs. It occurred to him, while shepherding Amelie back to bed, that he could curate a series of small selections—one for each member of the family. But the first will be for Amelie. He'll select sixty photographs—the funnier the better—one for each year of Dominic's photographic quest. He likes the idea that he might forge a new, deeper connection across the four generations. And the photo of the woman, dog and cigarette butts will make a fine opener for any series.

He looks up at the skylight. It's still black out there, but this time he notices Mars.

103

THE WASHING LINE

July

Toni Munroe sits in the garden studio—her dad's old studio—and dictates an address into a spreadsheet. The address is the current location of one of her dad's major commissions, a copy of Claude Lorrain's *The Embarkation of the Queen of Sheba*. She has confirmed the whereabouts of twenty-three of his paintings, but sixteen paintings still sit in the column titled *Location Unconfirmed*. Her dad kept pretty good records. Over the years, however, the paintings commissioned by private individuals have been handed down to their families, often moved to new residences or, Toni fears, chucked into storage. She wonders if some of her messages go unanswered because the owners don't want to admit they've lost the paintings. They're only copies after all. However, all his copies made for museum collections are still on display—these were among her dad's most lucrative commissions because the museums earned troves of money from touring the originals.

She looks across at the towels hanging, listless, from the washing line on this sunny, near-breezeless day, and smiles. She never relandscaped the back garden of her parents' home, for one reason: she retains a fractional memory of her mum pegging wet sheets to the washing line. She knows if her parents were looking down on her, they wouldn't mind if she made changes. However, Toni fears she might lose the memory if the garden were to take a different form.

It's a specific memory, not a generalized, woman-with-washing-basket-on-hip sort of thing. She sees a particular moment. A white sheet is pegged to the line; it's snapping back and forth in a strong wind. Her mum takes the weight of a second sheet—dark blue—on her shoulder and grabs the line with her left hand. She throws the blue sheet over the line with her right hand in a clearly practiced movement, and from her pocket she takes a wooden peg; she stabs it to the sheet. That exact movement is ice-cold clear—the way her mum stabs the peg on the line. All these years later, there's nothing so sweetly domestic to Toni's ear as the sound of violently flapping bedsheets. She loves a good drying day.

Toni says, "Add to my list of happy moments: Mum hanging out the laundry. And read the full list as it stands."

Her bracelet speaks in a voice carefully preferenced by Toni to sound like her friend Millie Dack—that is, to sound like Millie when she was a young woman.

"Bravo! You have twenty items on the list. May I suggest a few additional special moments based on your social history as—"

"No, no. None of that nonsense. Please, read the list."

"Would you like me to order the list chronologically?"

"No. In the order I thought of them." She leans back, folds her hands in her lap and closes her eyes.

The bracelet says, "One. When I pimped my denim jacket with embroidered cherry blossom and a Chinese sword.

"Two. My first story in the school newspaper.

"Three. Every time Atticus bakes bread.

"Four. When Marco was born."

"Pause," says Toni. She feels she ought to rank these happy moments, place Marco's birth at the top—one of *the* defining moments of her eighty-three years; the single life-defining event that displaced the loss of her mother. Toni's worldview changed on the day Atticus collected her and Marco from the hospital. As they walked out of the maternity unit, as she breathed fresh air after three days in the institutionalized, sanitized atmosphere of the postnatal ward, she grasped that everything had changed. The idea of Atticus living in a separate flat suddenly seemed preposterous.

She's on the verge of elevating Marco's birth to the top of her list, but she falters. The towels hang limp on the washing line; the breeze has died. It's uncanny; within that happiest moment—giving birth to Marco—a seed germinated for one of the deepest sadnesses of Toni's life. Marco never knew her mum. He grew up knowing Anna as his granny; children don't say *step-granny*, or do they? Marco should have called her *Anna*—Toni could have encouraged that. She should have reserved the granny title for her mum. Toni had hoped that as Marco grew up, he'd piece together bits of information, anecdotes about her mum, to create a picture of her, however distorted that picture was bound to be. But hard as Toni tried, dropping her mum's name into conversation whenever possible, she reckons Marco only truly *clicked* one afternoon in his twenties when the two of them were clearing up the kitchen. He'd made a roast dinner during a visit home; cooking was his hobby, how he relaxed. Toni told him that her mum, Connie—she always tried to imprint the name Connie on Marco's memory—had taken classes in French cookery in her spare time, that she'd considered going further. Toni had recounted this story before, but this was the first time he'd really listened. Marco asked, "Why didn't she go further?"

Of course, it was ancient history, but Toni did remember her mum saying, "I couldn't work all day in a hot kitchen."

It was Marco's reply that stays with Toni: "So it's your mum I take after, as much as anyone." In fact, hearing that simple statement is one of her happiest memories, but she won't add it to the list.

"Carry on," she says to her bracelet.

"Five. When I felt Millie's baby kick.

"Six. When Marco told me I'd be a grandmother, and when he brought little Amelie home.

"Toni, if I may interject—strictly speaking that's two separate items, but I'll continue.

"Seven. When Dad painted the bamboo graffiti.

"Eight. When Amelie was a toddler and started calling me Nan Toni."

She shudders with a silent laugh. Nan Toni and Gr'Atticus.

"Nine. When I moved into my first flat.

"Ten. When Dad took me to Shanghai Fabric Market.

"Eleven. When we moved back into Dad's house after he died.

"Twelve. Walking the walls of Xi'an city."

"Stop there," says Toni, for it strikes her as odd that three of these memories happened in the year after her mum's death. Toni realizes that if she and her dad hadn't travelled to China, she'd now see that entire year as a gaping black hole, a nothing time. To lose your mum at twelve years old was tragic by any standard, but to lose a loved one in the days before holographic reconstructions . . . Well, no one ever mentions that to Toni; it's too damned sad.

It isn't as easy as she'd thought to pinpoint the happiest moments in her life. Not because her memory is failing—it certainly isn't—but it requires chance connections to bring those happy moments to the forefront of her thoughts. She could make a list of her *unhappiest* moments in a trice. Why is that? Pain scrapes a deeper groove?

Amelie had prompted Toni's list-making—when she came over for Sunday lunch with Marco two weekends ago. Over puddings, they launched into their usual recounting of family tales. Toni told Amelie about that first visit to China, when she visited Suzhou—how she visited local gardens with exquisitely named pavilions—Putting a Question to the Spring Pavilion, the Pavilion of Dark Blue Waves. Amelie giggled when her Great-Grandad Dominic, sitting at the dining table in holo-mode, said, "Don't forget the Waterside Pavilion of Washing Hat Ribbons." He flickered. Anna, beside him, flickered too, as though a gust had blown across them both.

Amelie then asked Toni, "Was that the best time ever, Nan Toni? You know, the happiest? When you went to China with your dad?"

Toni, caught off-guard, found herself flustered. She summoned an unconvincing white lie, about *all* her life being happy. Amelie insisted, saying, "I'm serious, Nan Toni. I want to know your best day ever."

Funny little girl. Amelie Constance Munroe. Constance, after Toni's mum. She loves the old stories.

The end wall of the studio is hung with the abstracts Toni's dad painted during his retirement. Toni arranged the paintings this way after his death. They're still saleable, but Toni maintains they aren't hers to sell. They will belong to Amelie one day. And after Amelie, they will pass down hopefully along the bloodline, so that Dominic Munroe becomes the best-remembered ancestor in the family because there is *substance* to back up the family lore. She has already given Marco the digital files for her dad's street photography. She discovered these photographs after his death; it seems he'd worked on this unremunerated, personal project since his student days.

"Add another item to my list: When I discovered Dad's street photos."

She hears rain on the studio roof, but it's a passing shower; it lasts a couple of minutes. Perhaps her dad looked up from his work when it rained—checked if any sheets were on the washing line. Toni imagines him dashing out to the rescue, her mum rushing out from the house at the same time, and they're laughing as they throw pegs to the ground. They run, draped in sheets, back to the house.

Hardly anyone uses a washing line these days. Toni does so because she loves to repeat her mother's pegging action. And there's another reason. She loves the fact that even as an octogenarian she has the physical strength to lift the wet sheets. Thanks to her exo-skel. She and Atticus are early adopters in all things techy; she buys all the upgrades.

Her bracelet says, "Toni, you're scheduled for Nicol's skating class this afternoon, with Millie. Battersea Park. Do you need a nap before lunch?"

"Good idea. And remind Atticus that tonight's our date night."

She stands up from the desk and walks across the studio. She steps out of her exo-skel, then lies down on the narrow day bed. The bed is her addition to the studio, and she loves to wake up from a nap to the smell of pine cladding. "Wake me in forty-five minutes, will you?"

Toni relaxes in the luscious anticipation of an evening with Atticus. It's part of their understanding that they arrange a weekly date night whenever either of them has another love interest. He's been staying over with Candice for the past two months, but Toni reckons he'll return to her soon. No complaints though. She's been busy with her dad's archive, so, had Atticus been here, he might have felt neglected. And Atticus hasn't had a lover for at least five years, whereas Toni had a reunion last year with her old flame Freddie—returned home to England for his retirement. Freddie, thank God, has mellowed over the years. He's excellent company now; he's fun. And she still teases him about the theatre programmes; he'd always been pestering to complete his collection. She sent them eventually.

Freddie never had a family. In Toni's opinion, he was too self-absorbed in his youth, and quite frankly, too damned selfish. But she's let go of old aggravations, chats with Freddie most days, often before retiring for the evening. When Atticus is around, he joins in.

She hopes Atticus will tell her tonight that he's moving back. She misses the smell of his home-baked bread.

✕

Toni's one-seater pod delivers her to the centre of Battersea Park, an expansive space, the poorer cousin to public parks north of the river. It's a Londoners' park, south Londoners, that is. On a grey day, it feels desolate and uninviting, but on a bright day such as today, Battersea Park attracts as many runners, walkers, skaters, boarders, pram joggers and cyclists as any outdoor space in the capital.

As usual, Toni is the first club member to turn up; Millie is invariably the last. The group meets at two park benches opposite the Pump House Gallery. The tutor, Nicol, is setting out the games' paraphernalia. Toni's pod door slides open, and she steps out carrying her tote bag and skates.

"Look at you, all ready for action," says Nicol.

"We *are* skating today, aren't we?"

"Sure. Warm-ups, then twenty minutes skating around the park, and then a few games."

Toni drops her skates to the ground and reduces her exo-skel to medium assist. After all, zero effort means zero warm-up. This new suit is smarter than her last, so there's less chance she'll strain herself as she did last year. She missed all the summer sessions, even after two months of intense physio.

She starts her stretching routine, one that she's used ever since she lived in China. The People's Park in Shanghai had a mobile crèche, and twice a week she left Marco there while she joined a Tai Chi class of mainly elderly Shanghainese. She's pleased, even proud, that she also learned Mandarin, which she has kept up even though wearable translation is so much easier now.

She tips her head back, reaches her fingertips to the sky. Two birds are harrying a magpie—protecting their nest, no doubt. She stretches out to her left at shoulder height, holds it, then stretches to her right. In the distance, she sees three pods heading in her direction. One veers off towards the café pavilion. She continues her warm-up, stepping forward to stretch each calf in turn. Increasing the exo-skel assist, for it's too difficult otherwise, she takes her weight on her right foot, bends her left knee backwards and grabs her ankle with her hand. She stretches her thigh, counts to twenty before releasing, then does a right-thigh stretch. She bends from the waist, touches her toes. And, standing upright, she takes a long step forward and lunges, her back straight as a plank, then repeats. She feels energized.

She hears a pod door slide open behind her; she swivels around and waves. Millie slams the door closed and walks straight over to Toni, giving a perfunctory wave to Nicol. Toni embraces her friend. "Early for once?"

Millie's wearing her charcoal-grey sports gear with a lime-green skel, whereas Toni prefers her black skel, which merges well with most of her clothing.

"Tempted to cry off actually," Millie says, "but I needed to see you. I nearly buzzed you last night."

Toni continues with her warm-ups, as if trying to say, Look everything's normal, no need to stress. She twists at the waist, hands on hips, then throws her arms out to each side in turn to increase the stretch. "So what's the matter?"

Millie pulls sweatbands from her pocket, accidentally dropping one on the grass.

Nicol is approaching, so Millie replies abruptly, "I've hardly slept." She makes a half-hearted effort at her stretches, but her eyes are darting.

"You shouldn't be doing a session if you're knackered," says Toni.

Nicol reaches out, proffering her bracelet. Toni and Millie each touch their bracelets to hers—Millie showing one red light, and Toni showing two green.

"You're a bit below par, Millie. Don't overdo it today. Let me check you again after we've finished skating. You're fine, Toni."

Three more members of the group have arrived. Nicol walks away and calls over her shoulder to Toni and Millie, "Get started. Don't wait for everyone else."

"Is it Simone? Has she upset you?" says Toni as she snaps on her skates.

"No, it's Rudy."

"Come on. Let's chat while we're skating. Anyway, how's little Julia?" She knows the mention of Julia's name will lift Millie.

"Lovely as ever." Though Millie offers a smile, it's evidently an effort.

They set off together, but Millie struggles to find a rhythm. Toni drops her pace so they're able to skate side by side along the quiet stretch of path on the southern perimeter.

"I'm not thinking straight. I know you'll help," says Millie.

Toni accepts that she's Millie's mainstay. Millie's sister died four years ago, and in any case, Millie's never had the support that Toni's had from her own family. Through all the years of their friendship, Millie has run on half-empty. She's got Rudy, for sure, but you can't expect your children to prop you up. That's contrary to the natural order, Toni feels.

Up ahead, a pram jogger joins their path, so Toni and Millie skate on either side.

"After all these years. I can't believe it," says Millie.

Toni slows down. "What are you talking about? Spit it out, for heaven's sake."

"He wants to meet his biological father."

Toni takes Millie's hand and synchronizes to Millie's pace. "No way. I thought he wasn't bothered."

"He wasn't. I should have realized things would change. He's a father himself now."

"What did you say to him?"

"I kinda got upset, and then he started getting snarky"—her voice snags—"about how reckless I'd been to use a donor, that I'd known next to nothing about this man. I said, 'Well, everything worked out fine.

Look at yourself.' But he got irritable. He said *that* wasn't good enough."
In her agitation, Millie skates faster.

"But Rudy hasn't taken a conventional path himself. You used a donor, he went solo."

"Don't get me started. I only used a donor because I'd no other option. I told him so, and do you know what he said? He said, 'You didn't have to have a baby. The fact that *I'm here in the world* doesn't justify your decision.' I can't get over it. I can't sleep."

〉〈

After skating, the two friends bow out of Nicol's game session and slope off to the pavilion. Millie takes a seat, clearly downcast, while Toni fetches drinks.

"We didn't have a full-blown argument. We weren't shouting. I told him I knew enough about the donor to put my own mind at rest. The donors were all medical-checked *and* police-checked by the donor service that supplied the clinic. I specified a private-sector professional—preferably in engineering, because my grandfather was a draughtsman. I liked the idea of having some continuity, and I didn't want a medic like both my parents." She laughs. "Ridiculous, isn't it? I wanted to believe the donor didn't need the money, had a streak of altruism. But what did it matter, really?"

"Millie . . ." Toni shifts in her chair and lowers her voice. "What's the real reason Rudy wants to find the donor? Did you find that out?"

"He's been fact-checking about donor semen, researching the defunct operators and their processes, tells me the medical checks were never exhaustive. Some medical conditions develop in later life—could have happened to my donor. So he's decided to go ahead, find out if his father is still alive. Christ, he's already calling him his *father*. It makes me feel sick. Going back into all that. I mean, if I could have gone solo, like Rudy, I'd have jumped at the chance."

114

Toni struggles to say something helpful. Suddenly it seems she and Atticus did everything the simple way. "He sees everything differently, doesn't he?"

"I'm staggered; he waited until he was forty-seven. *And*, he wants to know if he has any half-siblings." She throws her head back and blinks away the tears. Then takes a deep breath and forces it out as though blowing out a candle. "You know, Toni . . . about Rudy and Simone . . . they've never explained why they have no contact at all with *her* family. I sometimes think there's a mass murderer on Simone's side."

※

That evening, Toni's mood lifts in the instant that Atticus pushes open the front door. He's carrying his suitcase. She doesn't fuss. She says, "Would you like to unpack before dinner?" He replies that he'll do exactly that. They hug one another as tightly as their exo-skels allow. She watches him climb the stairs. All these years. She sighs. They hadn't had the most romantic start to their lives together—a source of regret on her part—but that could have been the secret. No love bubble, no delusions. They've simply taken care of one another, allowed one another to follow an occasional romantic impulse. And, of course, they've always put Marco first. There's no easy explanation for their contentment.

She says, "Add to my list. Number twenty-two. When Atticus comes home."

LEAVE THE BABY TO CRY

September

Nancy needs to stand still, take a rest. Her calf muscles ache from walking along Brighton's pebbled beach. She knows her sister Nicol won't be flagging; she's as fit as a damned flea after running around Battersea Park all week. But then, keeping fit *is* her job.

So Nancy stops on the pretext of admiring a group of middle-aged women emerging from the waves breaking along the beach. As they battle against the waves' undertow, the bathers become stooped, their knees bent and feet splayed—closer to Neanderthal than *Homo sapiens*. They all wear black one-piece bathing costumes. Nancy assumes they're eccentric members of a club, committed to swimming in the sea every day of the year, whatever the weather. They're no longer tied to children or jobs, she reckons, and they've found a new physical challenge. It's their *thing*. Nancy imagines that when she reaches their age, she'll simply stay at home, catch up on forty years of films—feet up, cup of coffee and a comms auto-response: I'm afraid I can't talk just now. Please try later.

Nancy's admiration for the bathers morphs into a morbid inspection. People seem stripped of their personalities when their hair is plastered flat to their skull. She pouts. Humans are actually pretty ludicrous. During her last lesson on Friday afternoon, she taught fourteen-year-olds about species diversity in the tropics, taking frogs and toads as examples. Unsurprisingly, her pupils were repulsed by the sliminess of frogs and the wartiness of toads—"That's gross, miss." But looking at these bathers, Nancy sees that human skin isn't so beautiful; it's creased and roughened at every joint, sagging and seemingly splattered with its own warts, senile angiomas and liver spots. God-awful under a microscope, that's for sure.

Now Nancy sees that, viewed with detachment, a human head is an ugly thing, a form delivering multiple functions, a cavity in the face to accept fluid and organic matter—with a fleshy protuberance edging the entrance of that cavity, testing temperature and keeping the cavity airtight; a cartilage-supported protuberance to gather and filter inhalations; twin protuberances to receive sound waves. Inwardly, she recoils. How can one human be regarded as a better-looking specimen than another? She casts a glance at her sister, Nicol. Thick, glossy hair. Manicured and lithe. Even though Nicol carried her pregnancy, she resumed her pre-pregnancy shape within a few weeks of Clara being born. Of course, looking good is sine qua non for a fitness instructor; it's not imperative for a biology teacher. Nancy closes her eyes, feels the salt breeze prickle her skin. She's tired all the time these days. It's out of the question to start any fitness routine.

"I can't imagine getting an undisturbed night's sleep ever again," she says. "I can't remember what life was like before Timmy was born." She's annoyed with herself. Here they are, unencumbered for an hour while their partners entertain the kids on a beautiful sunny afternoon— a rare day trip to the beach—and so far they've talked about nothing *other than* their kids.

Nicol says, "I don't know how you can leave Timmy to cry like you do, Nancy."

Two elderly bathers, still in knee-deep water, reach out to one another and grasp hands. Evidently, if they were to be dragged under, they'd rather not be alone. Nancy feels dragged down herself.

"I'm out of bed at six fifteen, Monday to Friday. You can sleep in if little Clara sleeps late."

"That's not true. I've two early starts each week, and Saturday is *full on* for six hours in Battersea Park. From nine onwards with—"

"Timmy's not hungry, you know. He wakes up and wants to play. If we picked him up, he'd have us in and out of bed all night. And Sean is away every other week, so we have to be consistent. We can't pick Timmy up when Sean is here and *not* pick him up when I'm on my own. You're just lucky with Clara. If you have another . . . I mean, don't get me wrong, I wouldn't wish a bad sleeper on anyone, but next time you could have one like Timmy."

Nancy sets off walking before she's fully rested. Nicol catches up and says, "Sorry. I'm not criticizing. All I mean is, I don't know how you cope with the crying."

"Not much choice. And, don't listen to Mum. I know she says stuff—more than she says to my face. If she mentions my childbirth choices one more time . . ."

Nicol links their arms. "She doesn't understand. She carried her pregnancies; all her friends did too. Her main bugbear is your work ethic." She laughs. "Supremely ironic coming from a pushy parent."

"All that pushing, and now she complains I'm a workaholic. She's convinced I didn't carry Timmy because I was chasing a promotion. It's not true. It's bloody awful being pregnant in my job. I'm on my feet in class for six hours some days. Then I'm walking between the teaching blocks."

"How do other teachers manage?" asks Nicol.

Nancy doesn't like the sound of this question. She wants to believe that Nicol supports her against their mother, but maybe she shouldn't count on it. "They just do. That's their choice. But you remember Melissa in Chemistry? She came to my birthday party? She carried her pregnancy and then had horrible complications with haemorrhoids. She's still not right."

"That's unlucky."

"She was exhausted when she came back from maternity leave, but no one, absolutely *no one*, made any special allowance for her."

Nicol places her hand on Nancy's back. "You got so little maternity leave, Nancy, because you chose clinic gestation. I'd hate that. Didn't you want more time at home with Timmy before going back to work?"

"Well, yes. It would have been nice."

"So next time . . . ," says Nicol.

"There's no next time for us." Nancy feels tears coming and prays Nicol will let it drop.

"When you're older, Nance, I don't want you to feel you've missed out. It's lovely to carry your baby. You feel so . . ."

"Bonded. That's what you mean."

"I didn't say that."

"For Christ's sake. You're not being fair, Nicol. Stop putting this pressure on me."

"Don't get mad."

Nancy walks down towards the shoreline and stands there daring the waves to break over her feet. After a few moments, Nicol joins her, pulls her away from the waves. "Don't get wet." Nancy doesn't resist. They continue their stroll.

In measured words, Nancy says, "My Timmy would not be a better sleeper if I'd carried him. I know that's what Mum thinks."

"But you might not let him . . ."

"What? What? I might not let him cry? Bollocks. You agree with Mum, don't you?"

"Please don't get mad. We can talk about it, you and me."

Nancy and Nicol had learned during childhood that they could vent with one another—vent and move on. Clear the air, etcetera. They walk out of step for a couple of minutes. Nancy turns to her sister, asks how the skating sessions are going with the old folks. Nicol prises a smile out of Nancy, and then a giggle, admitting she can barely keep up with the old dears in their exo-skels. Nancy feels calmer, but the sound of pebbles grating underfoot keeps her earlier aggravation in play. And she knows herself too well; if, below the surface, a thought is niggling her, she's compelled to vocalize.

"I wasn't intending to tell you this, Nicol . . ."

Nicol raises her eyebrows. "Ominous."

"I had a chat with Dad last week. I didn't start it. I found him in his shed tinkering around. I think he was brooding on it when I turned up."

"Brooding? On what?" asks Nicol.

"He just came out with it. He said, 'I wanted more children, another one or two.'"

"What? I've never heard that before. He never talks about anything so personal."

"I asked if he'd always wanted a boy. If that was it. If he'd really wanted a boy. He said he simply liked the idea of a bigger family. So I said, 'Well, why didn't you have one?'"

"What did he say?" Nicol stops, sits down and reaches up to her sister. Nancy sits down next to her, close.

"He said it was Mum's decision. He couldn't persuade her. She didn't want to go through it all again."

"The sleepless nights?"

Nancy picks up a handful of pebbles, starts dropping them one at a time, as if she's weighing up whether she'll divulge the full story. Yes, she will. No, she won't. Eventually, "It wasn't the sleepless nights. He said that Mum couldn't face the pregnancy and birth. He said to me—there in his shed—that he tried to persuade her to use an artificial womb."

"No way! He didn't," says Nicol.

"Yep. He said she wasn't interested."

"It was new then."

Nancy drops the rest of the pebbles. "She wasn't scared or anything. He said she didn't like the idea of leaving the baby in the prenatal unit, leaving it in its 'little bottle,' as she called it."

"I suppose after she'd carried two babies, it wouldn't seem natural. So, does this explain why Mum gives you grief about your decision?" asks Nicol.

"That's immediately what I thought. I thought Mum rejected the whole idea and feels I was . . . *heartless*, leaving the baby in the hospital. Just visiting during gestation."

"I don't think—"

"But here's *the thing*, Nicol. Dad then said—believe me, I am not making this up—he said, 'I think she's having regrets. Seeing you. Seeing you and Timmy. And you feeling no guilt.' I think he wanted to cry. He said, 'We all have to live with our decisions.'"

JITTERY GOOD, JITTERY BAD

Amelie Munroe wakes up feeling jittery *good*—because her dad has finally agreed to take her to London, to Tate Britain—and jittery *bad*, because she may have chosen the wrong painting and the wrong museum. She sits up in bed and smacks the bedcovers with both hands. It's the right painting.

Last night, she considered asking her dad if *he* liked the painting, but she chickened out. Anyway, it's her private project, and she wants to keep it that way. It started with the art books she borrowed from Nan Toni—the ones with all the Madonnas. She found more Madonnas online, and now she has six pinboards, and she hasn't shared any of them. They're all marked secret. Earlier this week, Amelie checked every single page in the best of Nan Toni's books—*The Pre-Raphaelites*—and the painting on page 79 is the one she's going to see today. She told her dad she liked the "Pre-Raphs," which she knew sounded casual and amazingly au fait, but she didn't say which Pre-Raph painting she liked the best. After that brief conversation, she knows her dad's hoping she'll become a big-time artist like Great-Grandad Dominic, hopes she's following the family's special art interest. But her dad's not a real artist; he's an industrial designer.

She stretches and yawns. She needs to get in training for teenage years; communications with her dad should be strictly need-to-know.

✳

Marco takes Amelie's hand as they walk along the Embankment—away from the Houses of Parliament and towards Tate Britain. She skips.

"Excited?" he asks.

"Kind of." She swings her arms.

"It's great having a day out. I'm glad you didn't invite Bethany."

"That's really mean, Dad. Bethany has hardly any friends, and her mum is horrible."

"It's just nice to have a day together. You and me. We haven't done this for ages."

"Well, I've been *asking* you for ages."

Amelie had no intention of inviting Bethany. She'd be chatting all the time, and Amelie wants only her own thoughts in her head. She knows her dad will wander off around the gallery. He does that. Amelie supposes he wants his own thoughts too. Which is fair enough.

It bugs Amelie that Bethany is forever saying, "You're so lucky having a dad instead of a mum." But Bethany's mum is the odd one out. Amelie's other friends have lovely mums, some especially lovely. Emma's mum wears her hair in an elegant wrap like the Virgin Mary in *Madonna of the Meadow*. Amelie loves that picture. She found it in Nan Toni's *History of Western Art*. It shows Mary with two toddlers; they look like twins. But Amelie is far more interested in the painting she'll see today because it shows Mary with a biggish kid—Jesus, of course. People in the olden days were smaller, so Amelie classes the painting as a Madonna and Pre-Teen.

Her dad stops to look over the embankment wall at the river traffic on the Thames. "Fancy a boat trip later?"

"Er, yeah? S'pose."

124

She turns and makes a pirouette in the middle of the pavement. She's thinking about her pinboards, how she's going to reorganize all the images as soon as she gets home, and retitle each board:

Madonna and Baby Paintings
Madonna and Toddler Paintings
Madonna and Pre-Teen Paintings
Madonna and Child Advertisements
Madonna and Child Celebrities
Madonna and Child Films

Ж

Amelie is impressed. Her dad heads straight for the nineteenth-century galleries without checking the floor plan. How many times has he been here?

She knows that "the nineteenth century" means sometime in the nineteenth century, which begins *not* on the first day of 1900 but on the first day of 1800. After her first proper history lesson in high school, she told her dad, "If I say I'm in my twelfth year, then *surely* I'm twelve now."

He said, "That's wrong. If a baby is in its first year, it's zero years old. When you're twelve, you're in your thirteenth year."

And she said, "Well, you explain it better than my teacher did."

Amelie is wide-eyed as they enter the gallery. "It's all super-detailed, isn't it, Dad?"

"I can walk around with you, if you like. I know a bit about the symbolism. The meaning of the lilies is innocence, fallen leaves is about death, and a poppy—"

"I know all that. I'd rather look on my own."

"Let's play that game. Pick the painting you'd like to take home. Hmm?"

"Yeah."

Amelie wanders down the middle of the gallery as though she has no idea where to start. But she knows exactly where her painting hangs; she spied it as soon as they came in. It's on the right-hand side, halfway along the wall, on the lowest row. So lucky. She'll be able to stand right in front of it. She meanders along the left-hand wall of the gallery to kill time, because there's an old man standing in front of *her* painting.

She ignores all the labels because Nan Toni says you should decide for yourself if you like, or hate, a picture. You shouldn't need to know the title or the artist's name. Some people think that if so-and-so is the painter, it must be brilliant. In any case, Amelie is coming around to the opinion that it's not so difficult to become famous in the painting business. Once you paint one good picture, you're made for life. Especially if some important person buys the first one.

The old man is still standing in front of the painting as though he owned the damned thing. She wants him to move. And why is he so interested anyway? Unless he's religious. He must be a carpenter—he's wondering what Joseph is making on the workbench, what tools he's using, and checking if he's a neat worker. It's weird that this picture has two titles, because surely the painter said, "It's called *Christ in the House of His Parents*," or, "It's called *Christ in the Carpenter's Shop*." Did the person who bought the painting invent a second title?

The old man starts to move away, changes his mind and steps close up so that his nose is almost touching the painting. Amelie looks round to see if someone in charge is going to tell him off. He takes two steps backwards and walks away. Amelie grabs her chance; she stands in front of the painting with her feet planted wide apart, hands on hips, hoping to stop any adults from muscling in.

Joseph is making a door, which lies face down on the workbench. In front of the workbench is a scruffy Madonna—that is, Mary the Virgin. She's kneeling, and at first glance she seems to be praying, palms almost together. But Mary has curled her fingers inwards so that her fingernails are touching. She's definitely not praying. She's anxious about the boy, Jesus, who's standing next to her, leaning towards her so their faces are nearly touching. He's had a workshop accident—there's a trickle of blood in the palm of his left hand. He's holding up his palm like he's swearing an oath, and his right hand supports his raised arm at the elbow. It's a weird way to stand.

There's another boy, dark-haired, much better looking and stronger than Jesus, who seems a bit of a weakling. This other boy is walking around the end of the workbench with a bowl of water. He's taking a tiny step so he doesn't spill anything. Amelie knows the secret story here, the symbolism. The boy is John the Baptist, but he probably doesn't know it yet.

Amelie is not interested in John the Baptist. She looks all around the picture surface—like her dad taught her—but she's actually saving her gaze for the most important part of the painting as far as she's concerned. She steps closer and stares into the sad face of the Madonna. Jesus looks pretty calm about the whole accident. But his mother is frowning and tilting her face towards his. Their faces are close but not quite touching, as though he's so unbelievably precious he might break if their skin makes contact. Amelie steps back to look at Joseph's face. He's worried too. He's leaning over from the other side of his workbench. His right hand is touching Jesus's shoulder. But Joseph doesn't look anywhere near as anxious as Mary.

Amelie stares back at Jesus's face, Mary's face, their hands. It's like . . . it's like Jesus and Mary are oblivious to everyone else. No one else matters. Amelie nods to herself. Maybe mothers are best.

✗

Marco sets down a tray with tea and scones. "Well? Which painting are you taking home?" The café in the Tate's basement is crammed with chatter and the clashing of cutlery on crockery. Amelie slumps, feigning she hasn't any energy for the game. "I'm taking Ford Madox Brown's *The Last of England*," Marco says.

"Which is that one?"

"There's a man and woman, wrapped up in shawls. They're sitting at the back of a boat that's setting sail. They're wide-eyed, as though they're scared."

"Where are they going?"

"Australia. The artist made the painting after his best friend emigrated. They're scared about the long sea journey and because, I guess, they're worried they've made a bad decision. Then again, they probably had no choice."

She hesitates over adding a lump of sugar to her tea. "Why didn't they have a choice?"

"Short of work, most likely. That's why most people emigrated."

"If they don't like it in Australia, they'll come back to England, won't they?"

"Not in those days. One-way ticket."

"So that's why they look so worried?"

He nods. She sits back in her chair and frowns. "That's a big decision, isn't it?" They sit quietly as Amelie mulls over her dad's story, the story of the painting—a one-way ticket to the other side of the planet.

She sits forward and spreads butter across the cut surface of her scone.

"I know which painting you're taking home," says her dad.

"You don't."

"That one in the carpenter's workshop. I saw you looking at it. I like it too."

"Yeah. I like it."

"Why's that?" he asks.

"I just like it."

"That's not the game. You've got to say why."

"I like the two boys."

He laughs. "You serious?"

"No. I like the cosiness. They're all in the workshop, and they're all looking after Jesus, who's cut his hand."

Her dad says, "Did you notice—they all have dirty feet and dirty fingernails?" She shrugs. "People thought it was disgusting, disrespectful, when it was first exhibited. It had to be hidden away. Then a collector bought it, and Queen Victoria actually asked to see it—burning with curiosity, no doubt. So the painting became the talk of the town."

"That's mad. Because of dirty fingernails?"

"That was the whole point—to upset everyone. Shock tactics. The artist wanted everyone to see him as a modern painter."

⋊⋉

Amelie runs along the gangway of the riverboat, climbs the steps to the top deck and runs to the back of the boat.

"Come on," she shouts back to her dad. "Let's look over the back of the boat."

"Like the painting?"

"Yeah. *The Last of England*."

They stand at the back railing, watch the water churn as the riverboat pushes away from the landing stage and heads into the middle of the Thames. She imagines leaving London, knowing she'll never come back. Leaving her friends. They pass the Houses of Parliament and Big Ben. Marco puts his arm around Amelie. She turns and hugs him tight.

"Hey! What's the matter?" he says.

"Nothing. It's windy. Keep me warm."

"Have I been slow? A good-looking boy in a painting? I've an inkling . . . there's a cute boy at school?"

"No way. Don't be an idiot, Dad."

"Just wondering."

"Well, don't. Give your brain a rest."

※

As her dad opens the front door, Amelie ducks under his arm and runs up towards her bedroom. At the top of the stairs she twists around, looks down at him and says, as though prodded, "Thanks for the day out." And she's off again.

In her room, she lifts from her coat pocket the postcard she bought in the gift shop. It's the Madonna and Pre-Teen. She stands it on her bedside table, flops down on her bed and tries to copy the weird way Jesus is showing his bleeding hand.

It's not exactly the same thing as Jesus's workshop accident, but when she stayed off school with a sore throat, her dad took a day off work. He ran up and down the stairs bringing milkshakes and lukewarm soup—basically anything that wouldn't make daggers when she swallowed. Twice she had to bang on the floor for attention because he started watching cricket, which is why—she reckoned—he wanted to stay at home.

※

Amelie waits until Monday morning when she's in the car with her dad to ask the burning question. Sometimes you have to be brave. Make the big decision. She asks him as soon as he instructs the car—"School"— and before he opens his messages.

"Dad?"

"Hmm."

"Why did you make me, you know, on your own?"

"Blimey. I thought we'd gone through that."

"When? I don't remember."

"When you were smaller."

"I don't remember. Well . . . why did you? Why don't I have a mum?"

"Look, I have to drop you off in three minutes."

"Talk quickly, then."

He throws back his head. "Jeez, Amelie. I didn't need a mum. You know that."

"I know. But a gay dad can use a gifted egg. You didn't have to make your own."

"I thought it was the simplest thing to do."

"But why didn't you ask one of your friends to give you a few eggs? What about your friend Suzy? You've known her *forever*. Why didn't you ask her?"

"Amelie!" He takes her hand and squeezes. "A guy can't walk up to a woman and ask for an egg. It's not like placing a grocery order."

"You know what I mean. Why can't I have a mum like my friends?"

He's stumped for a couple of seconds. "You're all worked up, aren't you?" He pats her hand. "Let's talk it through after school. In a grown-up way. Okay?"

She nods. As they roll up to the school gates, he says, "You had two dads for a while."

"Colin wasn't a parent though, was he? Just a boyfriend."

"But he still comes to see us. It's *you* he misses."

"Well, he doesn't count. And I don't miss him."

"But you do like him. When he visits, the two of you are always laughing." He tickles her gently in the ribs with his forefinger.

Amelie can't stop herself. She grins. "Yeah, I know."

"Okay then?"

"Yeah. See you later."

⋊

Amelie feels jittery bad all day at school. In geography, her teacher asks a question about glacier calving; no one knows the answer except Amelie.

She doesn't raise her hand because someone might notice the red pen mark she's scribbled in her palm.

During their afternoon break, she tries to scrub off the red mark. Her friend Emma is hanging around by the sinks. Amelie shifts so her friend won't see the stupid stigmata. Emma is oblivious and asks her if she wants to come round to her house when classes finish. Amelie says, "Can't."

"Go on. You can stay for dinner."

"Can't. Dad's expecting me home."

Truth is, she doesn't want to see Emma's perfect mum in her perfect headwrap. Not today, anyway. She says, "Come on, let's have a walk around outside."

The best thing about walking around the playing field is that no one can listen in. You can talk about who you fancy and who you hate. After they've dismissed half the boys in their year, mainly for being pathetically juvenile, Amelie says, "You know when you had that sore throat, the one I caught off you?"

"How do you know you caught it off me?"

"Only joking."

"Well, what about it?" asks Emma.

"Did your mum stay home? Give you loads of attention?"

"My mum? Take a day off work? She never does that. She dumped me at my gran's. I got even *sicker* because I had to listen to Gran's putrid music and eat her disgusting pea and ham soup. Why do you want to know?"

Amelie didn't like to say, so she improvised. "You only took one day off school. I had a Friday off, but I was still sick over the weekend. So my sore throat was worse than yours."

"No it wasn't. I told my mum I was well enough to go back to school. But I wasn't."

⋇

When Amelie arrives home, there's a message alert on the kitchen wall: *Won't be late, picking up takeaway.* She loves an early meal. Her dad knows that. Whereas, at Emma's, they have to wait until her older sister gets home, and she's alpha sporty, so it gets ridiculously late.

An hour later, her dad rushes into the kitchen and pushes the takeaway across the worktop. He always does that. Like he's a barman in a cowboy film, sliding a glass of whisky.

"Hungry?" he says.

"Dad?"

"Come on, get the plates out, Amelie. I'm starving."

She stoops to lift plates out of the cupboard. "I'm sorry about this morning."

"No need to be. We should talk more, but not when I'm hungry." He laughs.

"I don't need to any more. I just want you to know, I think about it sometimes."

He's unpacking the takeaway. Chinese—her number one favourite. "You're bound to. I'm always happy to chat. Anyway, I've got some news."

"What?"

"I've asked my friend Suzy to come on holiday with us this year."

Amelie hugs her dad, then charges off. She runs up the stairs. He calls after her: "Where've you gone? Amelie!"

In her room, she picks up the postcard of the Madonna and Pre-Teen from the bedside table and leaps across to her desk. She opens the desk drawer, then lingers to gaze once more at Mary's sad, creased face. She'll get over it. Amelie chucks the postcard in the drawer, slams the drawer shut and calls up her Madonna pinboards—because it's time for a big decision.

"Delete all," she says.

THE RIGHT THING TO DO

I'm looking out for Rudy Dack—it's our first face-to-face contact. He's always known that he's a donor-conceived child.

Before I meet one of my offspring, I ask, straight-out: "When did your mother tell you?" That way I'm prepared.

I've positioned myself at a good vantage point; I can monitor anyone approaching the café. I've taken a table in the outside eating area, in the shade of a scarlet oak, one of the more unusual trees in St. James's Park.

It's my theory that a mother will wait, more often than not, seven or eight years before making the big revelation about her child's true parentage. She waits, I reckon, until the child has lost the cherubic looks of infancy, and then asks herself: Will this child pass as my own? In my experience—now that several of my children have come calling—the longer these parents delay in making their revelations, the more screwed up the children are in the long run.

One of my offspring coped just fine even though his mother broke the news well into his adulthood. In that instance, I assumed he'd inherited placid genes from his mother because I'm sure, in his position, I'd be angry. Really angry. I mean, everyone wants to know where they come from.

So, here I go again. It's several years since the last one, and quite frankly I wasn't expecting to meet any more. I'm a bit niggled. Why has it taken Rudy so long to make contact? I haven't asked him yet. I've learned it's best to talk about personal motivations at the first meet-up, when we can read one another's facial expressions and body language. Potentially, it's a volatile moment, though I've never encountered any awkwardness I couldn't handle. Ha! I should be a psychiatrist.

I've arranged our meeting in St. James's Park because I'm in London for a couple of days' meetings and the weather forecast is good. I find, after the initial small talk, it's easier to get into deeper issues while taking a stroll, when we're not looking directly at one another. Especially with a man. But then, they're all different.

Personally, I *wouldn't* choose Rudy as a name, and I'm sure my wife wouldn't either. If Kas *had* suggested Rudy as a name, I'd have applied the veto. She applied the veto on my suggestion of Hermione. That's what I like about these reunions. Well, reunion isn't the right word, is it? Let me put it this way: I like the surprises—not simply the oddity of their names, but their accents, their religions, their manners, how they dress. And their jobs, of course. I've been caught off-guard a couple of times. I wasn't prepared for the tattooed girl. Nor the lad with extreme views on healthy lifestyles—a bit too keen to convert me.

Perhaps Rudy will be the child I truly click with. I'm curious—it's only natural—to see if they look like me or have a mannerism that I recognize. The health-fanatic guy had exactly the same laugh. That was strange. But I've yet to meet a son who's a younger version of me. I might even have a *daughter* who's a female version of a younger me—she's out there in the world, not knowing that I'm her father. Over the years, I've spoken with other sperm donors who say they've encountered such offspring, chips off the old block. Out of so many children, you'd think I'd find one, but it hasn't happened yet, and maybe it won't now.

My next-door neighbour's children favour their mother; they seem to spring from her side of the family—looks and personality—as though her husband has one hundred per cent recessive genes. Are my genes mostly recessive?

From my official donations—I don't know how many babies were conceived in total—I've met five of my children, and I remain in contact with four of them; the fifth was satisfied to meet me the once, to check my medical history. She said, quite correctly, that the pre-screening can't identify all the genetic faults. Fortunately, I've remained healthy, and I've looked after myself. No medical surprises—that's what they all want to know. I sometimes feel bad about my unofficial donations because I can't tell the recipients that I'm still fighting fit. I could place myself on an informal donor register for the sake of those women and their kids, but Kas doesn't know about my *unofficials*, so it's best to keep a low profile.

When Kas and I were getting serious—that is, when we planned our first holiday together—I told her about the official donations. She wasn't too concerned, most likely because she wasn't sure we'd last; she wasn't completely invested in me at that point. I think she was impressed that I waived the donor fee. She said, "At least you know you're not firing blanks." That's Kas for you. She's keen on action films, reads up on survivalism, the post-apocalypse. That's why she was keen I took the posting outside London. She wanted to live in a rural area, without being too rural. Apparently, that's one of the ground rules for surviving Armageddon. Well, there's no harm in it, I suppose, and I admit I enjoy being more self-sufficient. The vegetable garden is my responsibility, and it's remarkably good for stress relief.

Initially, I was taken aback when Kas chose remote gestation for our baby. I'd assumed she'd embrace the earth-mother thing—back to nature, self-sufficiency, etcetera. But she wanted to ensure our child had the best start, had the best chance of *surviving*. In her eyes, that meant tidying up his or her genome by going for IVF and an artificial womb. I was all for it! A robust child. Why carry forward the full load of genetic mutations if you can avoid it?

Kas hasn't told her family about my other children.

I didn't risk telling her the full story about my unofficials. She'd accepted the concept, so what did it matter? My intentions were honourable. But I don't think she'd want to know that I donated to sixty-three more women over a three-year period. It was roughly one a month initially, but as word got around, it escalated so that I was doing a handover almost weekly. That became a bit crazy, so I stopped.

I learned much later that these unofficials could have claimed child support from me—being off-piste, without contracts. I told each of these women it was best to apportion fatherhood to a one-night stand, someone she'd never see again. We had these conversations over cappuccinos, always out of town so no one would recognize me. You know, with a strange woman. Towards the end, I had to ask for travel expenses because it was making quite a dent in my beer money. Truth is, they'd have met me *anywhere*—I suppose the Darwin Centre café would have been the most appropriate—because I had what they all wanted. Fully compliant, medically approved sperm. I showed them the approval form from the clinic, verifying the quality of my sperm, and my latest STD certificate.

The alternative, for my cappuccino women, was an unscreened supply—a plastic pot and a syringe, from some guy who'd probably made hundreds of donations for fifty quid a shot—handed over outside the toilets on a railway platform or in a multi-storey car park. I saved them from that grim scenario.

So today, I'm meeting Rudy, my sixth official donor-sperm-conceived child. Probably my last such encounter. I've looked closely at the statistical evidence, and I reckon I've several other children out there, but most likely they're entirely unaware of the circumstances surrounding their conception.

X

Here goes. This looks like Rudy, approaching the outdoor seating at the café. He's looking around, but he's cool about it. I've come to recognize when people are meeting for first dates, which is what this is in essence. They've seen photographs of one another, but photographs can give the wrong impression—some people look taller, or shorter, in real life. Or it's immediately obvious they're stoic, shy types. Or excitable, fidgety types—you don't often see that in a photograph.

My God, he walks like me—a swagger without looking tough. Just confident. I stand because it's not appropriate for *me* to act cool. I wave him over, and as he approaches, I smile and offer a handshake. I'm reminded: the only wealth in this world is children. He seems hesitant. I might be smiling too much. He grips my hand and says, "I didn't expect a Mafioso don." We both laugh, and I know this is going to go well. "It's the white shirt and black suit," he says. He sits down before I do.

"Ah, yes." I look down at my clothes. "I've come straight from a conference." I wonder if he's slighted; I'm killing two birds with one stone in visiting London. "It's a coincidence, Rudy. After we arranged to meet, I noticed an old friend would be speaking at the conference. So . . ." I shrug. "It's good to meet you."

A waiter comes across. Rudy orders a double espresso.

We sit quietly. I wait for him to speak. We've covered the basics in our messages—where we live, our work, the people we share our lives with. We already know we have some similarities; we both have an engineering bent, but whereas I went into flood defences—he's suitably impressed I worked on the Second Thames Barrier—he went into aeronautics.

Often I start by asking why my offspring wanted to make contact, but it doesn't feel right with this guy. As though reading my mind, he says, "You see, my mother raised me on her own. My mother's older sister, who lived with us, has died. Her brother too. And my wife is estranged from her parents and siblings. We've no other family. It feels . . . lacking, you know?"

"I can see that. But I'm not sure I can offer you a bigger family."

We sit in silence again. I have to be careful not to raise his expectations. I certainly won't take him home! But I can offer a consolation prize. "I can put you in touch with some of my other donor-conceived children. They're in contact with one another, and I believe they meet regularly. Two men, two women. They'll welcome you along if you're interested."

The waiter returns with the coffee. Rudy pays, and when the waiter's out of earshot, he asks, "How many kids do you have? Do you even know?"

"I have a rough idea. I had to stop donating—that was the law—when I'd created ten families, sometimes more than one child in a family. I guess I've fathered up to fifteen children."

"But it could be more?"

"I'm not privy to the information. Six of my children, including you, Rudy, have come forward to contact me—and I've met them all. And according to the studies I've read, more than half of donor-conceived offspring never make contact."

"And you only ever donated through the clinic?"

"Hey, look. The sun's out. Drink up and let's take a walk."

We head towards the footbridge, and I make small talk about how many years I've been coming to this park, how I've seen the park in snow just once. When we reach the middle of the bridge, I stop and say, "Tell me, Rudy. Why have you waited so many years to meet me? I suspect you'll be the last one. This is a very special day for me."

"I've always known. I can't remember any specific moment as *the moment* my mother told me."

"That's how it should be. I'm pleased to hear it."

"I held back because I didn't want to hurt her feelings, and I'd never go behind her back. As I said, there's me and her." He leans on the bridge railing. "Actually that's not quite true. I'm close to my godfather, Aiden, and I talked it over with him before I told my mother."

I'm relieved to hear this. I like to know there's someone standing in for me in my children's lives. I'm not saying my stand-in should be a man, but I'm relieved when there's someone who acts as a mentor, or at least acts as a listening post. That's how I like to act in my own family, as the type of father who makes time for his children, who listens, and who offers advice but only when it's asked for. A father should show reticence because his advice could be entirely wrong. Because your children aren't you, are they?

I'm already warming to Rudy, and I have to admit I feel a pang. I wish he'd contacted me at a younger age.

Rudy says, "I don't look anything like my mother. She has loads of framed photographs of her relatives—dead before I was born, most of them—and I don't look like any of *them* either. I'm here partly out of curiosity." He looks me up and down, stares hard into my eyes as though he's trying to scrape the inside of my skull. I've seen that look before. He cocks his head and says, "But now I see the similarity, it doesn't seem such a big deal."

"That's a healthy attitude, Rudy."

"I wanted to meet you, mainly, because I'll want to tell my daughter about my donor conception. At some point. She's a baby. But when she's older, when I tell her, she'll want to know if I ever met you. So I'm doing this so I can answer her questions. If you won't take offence, my main hope is that she'll see her own conception as preferable to mine. She's my solo daughter—all her DNA is mine. I want her to feel that being a solo child is better than being a donor-conceived child."

Well, I could take offence, but it's my responsibility to rise above that. "Your mother must have longed for a child, Rudy. You've brought a lot of happiness to her, and after all, you're here in the world, aren't you? That's got to be a good thing. You seem like a fine person—"

He cuts me off. "You didn't answer my question: Did you make donations to any women other than at the clinic?"

141

"Look, that's not why we're meeting." I'm calm, but my back is prickling. "Your godfather—tell me about him."

He takes a deep breath, releases it suddenly. "That's another mess. My mother doesn't know I'm aware of it, but Aiden told me—my mother wanted *him* to be the donor."

"Why didn't he? He's clearly a big part of your life, and your mother's life I'd guess."

"They *were* in a relationship. He said he was young for his age, immature, and couldn't understand why my mother was in such a rush. He didn't even object when she went for treatment at the clinic. But when she announced she was pregnant, it seems he went into a tailspin. Realized he'd been stupid. He put on a brave face, he said, but he didn't stick around—couldn't bear to see her belly expanding. He took off travelling. When, eventually, he came back, my mother asked him to be my godfather. She isn't one to bear a grudge, and I think she missed him."

"Godfather rather than father. And he's still filled with regrets?"

"I don't think so. Not any more. He takes the view that donor conception was a bad phase we went through—that the whole idea was flawed, from the children's point of view."

He turns and sneers. Sneers at *me*. I can't believe it. Here he is, a big handsome guy, like *I* used to be. He says, "I have to agree with my godfather. It's a total existential fuck-up."

I can't help it—my shoulders twitch. Rudy should be mad at this *Aiden*, or his mother, not with me.

Reading my thoughts again, he says, "I'm not angry, exactly. I'm sad, because Aiden's explanation made a barrier between me and my mother. She couldn't see past her own needs—what *she* wanted." Rudy reaches across and places a hand on my shoulder. He's two or three inches taller than me. "Well? Did you donate to other women?"

"Once or twice."

His hand grips my shoulder. "You can *surely* remember if it was once or twice? Don't bullshit me, man. You've done hundreds, haven't you? And they'll be my age, and they've had children, and those children are spread all over the place. What if my Julia meets one of them in later life, and they seem to have a lot in common? Damned *likely* if they're related. What happens if they fall for one another?"

"No, no! Not hundreds. I helped a few women who couldn't afford the official route, and they had the peace of mind that I'd been vetted. I never did it for the money. You've got to believe me—it felt the *right* thing to do at the time."

He walks away from me. I have to decide if I should end it here or if I should follow him. I follow. He takes the path leading into a woodland walk, and I suddenly feel belittled—by this younger version of myself. I mean, he's not being fair, or practical, at all. I want him to see that. I'm a pace behind him when I say, "You're different to the others, Rudy. I can feel it. You're so much like me."

He stops dead in his tracks, twists around. "It's all about you, isn't it? So fucking arrogant."

I reach out to him. He brushes my arm away and steps back. He says, "You know, I'm so happy to have *one* child. But that wasn't enough for you, was it? You had to impregnate hundreds of women."

"It wasn't like that, Rudy. Give me the benefit of the doubt. The fact is . . . if Aiden had agreed to father a child with your mother, then you wouldn't *be* here."

Rudy half turns. His body twists, and a fist swings at me. My jaw cracks—Jesus! I'm on my back. Blood filling my mouth. I try to haul myself up on one elbow. Rudy! I look for him, desperately. He *is* the one.

PART THREE

2120

BABY BERTRAND HOUSE

March

Staring at the word *Gerard*, piped in pale blue icing on a chocolate-coated cake—cook had given him a choice of chocolate or buttercream—he said, "I hate my name. It's too serious."

Mrs. Bourne-Boyd, his caregiver at the Bertrand House boarding academy, replied that his mother didn't choose his name. "She's not to blame," she said emphatically. "Sadly, dear, your mother died before she'd decided what to call you. But when I went to collect you from the gestation clinic, one of the technicians had written *Gerard* on your crib." Apparently, there'd been a delay with the insurance papers, and the technician couldn't bear to see the orphan labelled *Baby Bertrand House*.

This revelation came on the occasion of his ninth birthday. Gerard can still feel the weight of Mrs. Bourne-Boyd's hand on his shoulder as she added, brightly but unhelpfully, "You could always call yourself Gerry."

Oh, sure. Gerry Rossi, sounds like a bare-knuckle fighter.

He has since learned that Gerard is the patron saint of expectant mothers. This seems a doubly inappropriate name in his own case; his mother outsourced her pregnancy, and no saint saved her from her cycling accident. He imagines the hospital technician as a white-haired, confused religious zealot. Anyway, why would a male saint take the mantle of protection over expectant mothers?

As a reaction to his dull name—*Gerard*—he's careful about his appearance: he's a sharp dresser. Checking himself in the bedroom mirror, he decides he should open the neck flaps of his perfectly moulded top. That's all it takes. Smart, just short of too neat, and as ever, no brand labels. He's a brand consultant, and he doesn't want anyone to judge him based merely on his shopping preferences. He knows how easily people are swayed. His wife, Scarlett, has often teased him over this yen for anonymity. She suggests it's an affectation, verging on phobic. For all that, she willingly adopts the same no-brand policy for their son. They spell it out for Louis in terms a bright five-year-old can understand: it isn't polite to be a show-off. Just because they can afford nice clothes, nice stuff, they shouldn't rub it in anyone's face. It's what you *do* in life, how you treat others, that makes you an attractive person.

Gerard leaves their family home, nestled in affluent Belsize Park in north London, and sets out on his annual half-day pilgrimage. For the past decade at least, on his birthday, he has strolled southwards, picking his route through as many parks as possible to Bertrand House. He sits in the grounds of his childhood home, takes stock of the past year and considers the year forthcoming. He goes alone; it's not a family outing—it's too long a walk for Louis.

Scarlett understands that Gerard needs this quiet time. She once said: "It's your day. You should do as you please." In any case, he doesn't want his annual stroll to be one more commitment in her permanently squeezed schedule. He wouldn't want her fretting, if she were to accompany him, about jobs piling up. This is *his* birthday ritual—tracing, in reverse, the journey he made from his parentless upbringing to his middle-class success.

He doesn't look back on his childhood as an unhappy one—in some ways it was the best time of his life. However, he's aware he could use his upbringing as an easy excuse for fucking up. Until this year, he hasn't needed one.

)(

He stands at the top of Primrose Hill looking down towards Regent's Park and central London. At this time of the day—the air fresh and dewy, more so than in any metropolis he has ever visited—he can imagine the meadowlands of previous centuries, the grazing cattle, the sheep. He's proud that London has preserved its green spaces. The walking commuters who use this park as a cut-through to the West End are already at work in their offices. The stream of early-morning runners has reduced to a trickle, replaced by the pram pushers—well-to-do local residents, or the droids of well-to-do residents—out and about with their beloved offspring.

Gerard's good humour, however, is ever so slightly marred; Dr. Kristina Christophe has not sent him a birthday message. He suspects she isn't allowed to contact her clinic babies now that she's retired. He went to her leaving party last year at the clinic, and he doubts he'll be going there again.

Every year, Dr. Christophe had held a soirée at her own home for those in her select group—as she called it. Those who were orphaned while in gestation. He wonders if these gatherings will be discontinued. He has often suspected that Dr. Christophe played Cupid at her soirées; she wanted to be sure they were happy, as though she felt party to their tragic start in life. But she shouldn't have felt bad—they were all insured risks. Well insured.

Dr. Christophe came to their wedding. She expressed her delight to Gerard that young people still believed in marriage. And she approved of Scarlett. Gerard knew why—he'd married up the gene pool. Scarlett's

149

parents had gone further than a standard clean-up of the mutation load. Scarlett is effortlessly supersmart and sleek.

Gerard picks up his pace and allows his arms to swing as he walks down the steep path through the park. There's nothing to stop him contacting Dr. Christophe, he reckons. He needs to talk with someone who won't judge him, who will give him the benefit of the doubt. To his mind, Dr. Christophe has seen it all before; she seems unshockable, as though no manner of errant behaviour lies beyond her imagination. He's sure she won't ever change.

$$\mathbb{X}$$

An hour and a half later, having kept a steady pace through the back streets of Marylebone and Mayfair, picking a route through Green Park, then St. James's Park, and crossing Westminster Bridge towards Archbishop Park, he finally arrives at the orphanage, not far from the Imperial War Museum. No one ever refers to Bertrand House as an orphanage, but Gerard knows a branding exercise when he sees one.

He sits on the wooden bench he donated to Bertrand House, positioned as he'd requested, next to the rhododendron border. Five years ago, one of the trustees—a keen gardener it seems—argued that the rhododendrons should be rooted out. Fortunately, the two trustees who were former residents slapped down the idea; they didn't see the border as overgrown shrubbery, of little horticultural merit. They saw a thicket, a jungle, a place for adventure, for expeditionary forces led by nine-year-olds, young boys and girls hacking through with wearable virtual machetes.

Gerard surveys the scene, checking that the quirkiness of the gardens remains untamed: the den below the low-hanging boughs of a weeping purple beech; the overburdened rose trellis, a demarcation line between warring tribes. He sees a droid gardener in the distance, tending the vegetable plots. To the children, these plots formed the centrepiece of a survivalist community, struggling in the aftermath of an apocalypse. The nature of the apocalypse changed from day to day, according to their whims, but the consequence was a constant—all the adults were dead; the children had to grow their own food.

It's eighteen years since he left Bertrand House. He mentors five former residents, and he attends the alumni parties and career days. There's no excuse for any child not to do well; they've had every advantage. As clinic orphans they've all benefited from some degree of genetic enhancement. Their caregivers at Bertrand House were well paid and affectionate. Class sizes were small, and each child had his or her own life coach.

That's exactly what he needs—a life coach to sort out the one and only fuck-up in his adult life.

He'll have to tell Scarlett. He doesn't think she'll be too upset; it's history. But she might be upset by the financial implications. He finds it difficult to second-guess her reaction. Will she pity the boy, want to help him?

He can't conjure the woman's face. He hadn't remembered her name. Freya Liddicoat, as it happens. Gerard and Freya. Doesn't sound right. He remembers standing at the beach bar waiting to order another round of drinks. He and his mates, after a perfect day of surfing, had probably downed a few pints by that point. The sun was low. It lit the bottles behind the bar—one of those moments when, as a young man, he knew life was good. She came out of the kitchen, pulled two pints, and while waiting for the froth to settle, she reached up and removed her hair grips. Her red hair fell in long crinkles around her face. His one lasting impression. Her hair alight in the setting sun. But he still can't see her eyes, her mouth. He told her they were having a party later on the beach, and why didn't she join them? She said she would. He can't remember any conversation, maybe they didn't talk much, but they exchanged profiles. They had sex on the beach. It was pitch-dark. The sex is no more fixed in his memory than a dream. But he sees her hair, from the bar.

It was afterwards he felt embarrassed about the hook-up; it soon became obvious that she was ten years older than him, at least. So, after a month, he muted their connection, and not long after *that*, he blocked her. Evidently, she had kept tabs on him from a distance. She closed in last week, sent a message to his work address. At least she didn't turn up in person.

The kid is eleven years old. *Skye*, for heaven's sake. Skye Liddicoat. Gerard, Freya and Skye? Not a likely combination. And she *carried* the pregnancy. No interventions at all, a raw birth, and an unprivileged upbringing, from what he's gathered. She isn't a fundamentalist or some weirdo; she just doesn't have money. She's poor and she's come knocking, asking for help with the kid's education, saying he can't reach his full potential. Whatever that might be. Lord knows. Poor little blighter.

Now they've exchanged a few messages, he realizes his initial error. He had assumed, at the beach bar, that she was a student with a summer bar job. But she was permanent bar staff. Over the years, she's moved from one menial job to another, so what chance does the kid have?

He looks up at the top floor of Bertrand House. It's still a playroom for those wet days when the children are cooped up. His memory conjures the sound of a Ping-Pong ball hitting bat and table, at a child's stuttering pace.

What did Freya think she was doing, keeping the baby? Why didn't she chase him for support years ago? He could have taken the boy off her hands, paid for postnatal improvements, enrolled him in a suitable school. She has completely wrecked the boy's chances. And he suspects she's holding back, that there's something else she isn't telling him, but he's not sure how much he wants to know. He replied to her initial message, saying they should meet, that he wanted to meet the boy. He also pointed out that she ought to have told him she was pregnant; he had the right to know, if not legally then at least ethically speaking.

The upshot: next week, he's meeting her halfway, in Bristol.

The droid gardener pushes his wheelbarrow to the green waste and tips out the pile of weeds. He backs up, then pushes the wheelbarrow along the rhododendron border and sets to work on the rose bed in front of Gerard. The gardener says, "Good morning. Am I disturbing you?"

"No. Carry on," says Gerard. He wonders why Bertrand House specified a male droid. The original gardener was a woman—Dora, strong as an ox. She worked here well into her seventies.

The droid paces each side of the rectangular bed, his head turned as he scans the scattering of weeds and the roses, their buds still closed tight.

"You don't need those overalls, do you?" says Gerard.

"Better to be safe than sorry." He unhooks a laser from his tool belt and fires at each weed. He refixes the laser to his belt and takes an insecticide pen, sidesteps around the bed, applying the pen spray over each colony of aphids.

Gerard wonders what kind of job Freya's boy can hope for. He'll have to operate within a small business that can't afford a droid. But what? Bar work, kitchen work, like his mother?

❋

The following day—he didn't want to taint his birthday—he informs Scarlett about the boy. And her first comment: "So, he's your elder son."

He manages to stop himself saying, But he doesn't really count. Rather, he says, "Perhaps it would benefit Louis to know his half-brother. It could bring out the caring side of his personality. At five years old, the difference between him and Skye won't be stark. A few years from now, it will be too late." He knows he's being romantic. Most likely, it would be embarrassing for everyone even at this stage; they'd all note the subtle differences. And even though Freya's boy is bound to be physically bigger, Louis's mental dexterity would be apparent to everyone.

Ж

Gerard arrives twenty minutes early at their agreed rendezvous, as though to emphasize that even though he's an absentee father, he can still be relied upon for punctuality. He suggested the quayside of Bristol's dry dock because it's the final resting place for the SS *Great Britain*. He thought the ship would provide a good talking point. He can tell the boy about the ship's history—the first ocean-going ship built of iron—about its screw propeller, and how the owners paid a high price for innovation: frequent repairs, structural changes to stop the yawing motion, which made all the passengers seasick. But maybe Skye isn't interested in engineering. Gerard decides the ship's chequered history will be far more interesting to the boy than simply saying it was the best, the biggest, the fastest.

And the ship had a happy ending, eventually. After decades of carrying passengers to New York and Australia, it was converted to sail and transported coal, later becoming a quarantine ship and finally a coal bunker in the Falklands. But that wasn't the end of the SS *Great Britain*. True, it had been scuttled and abandoned in Sparrow Cove in the Falklands, but it won redemption when it was towed back to Bristol for renovation.

Gerard is pleased with his plan, but he's far from relaxed. He paces back and forth along the quay, avoiding the shadows of moored vessels, for the breeze has a cold nip. Freya Liddicoat has been polite, measured, in her messages, but she might be quite different face to face. Hopefully, the boy's presence will temper any agitation she might be feeling.

He sees a woman in the distance who could be Freya, but she's alone, no boy. As she approaches, he feels a thudding in his chest. Her hair is the giveaway, though a little dulled and shorter than he remembers. He doesn't gesture until she smiles. She reaches out to shake hands. Her grip is confident. He's relieved she doesn't attempt to hug him. "Thanks for being early. I dreaded a no-show," she says. "And thanks for sending the train fares."

His gaze flicks away from her face to her coat. He takes in the high-end brand and the poor quality of the coat seams. It's a cheap rip-off.

"Where is he?" asks Gerard.

She glares at him.

"Sorry. I mean, hello, and . . . where's Skye?"

"He'll be along in half an hour. I've travelled up with a friend—she's taken him for an ice cream."

"So we can talk?"

"Yes, out of earshot. I've told him I'm meeting an old friend, nothing more than that."

"I've bought tickets for the museum ship." He digs them out of his pocket and points to the SS *Great Britain*. "I thought he'd like to explore belowdecks." He pushes his hands back into his pockets. "Will you tell him afterwards? That I'm his dad?"

"Depends. Let's see how it goes."

※

Gerard and Freya walk in step along the deck. Gerard stops and touches the crook of her elbow. They face one another. "You do realize, Freya, I'd no choice. I had to do the DNA test."

"Course you did. A one-night stand. I've had a few, and I'm sure you have too."

He says, more abruptly than intended, "I'm settled now." They both fall silent, and Gerard is tempted to turn and bolt. Who is this woman, he asks himself? Is she a fit mother? Is she a bit dim, or what? He can't tell much from her accent; there's a pleasant-enough lilt. "Why didn't you tell me you were pregnant?" he asks.

"Well, for one thing, you blocked me, didn't you? I was pretty pissed off about that, but then . . . well, I got into a spot of trouble, if you *must* know. So I didn't bother tracking you down." She laughs. Gerard freezes. Her laugh sounds coarse to his ear. There's a cackle within it. "As if I wasn't in enough trouble already." Her smiles slides away. "The pregnancy started to show, you know?" He looks away, inwardly shrinks, for he never thought a child of his would start life *on board.* "Some busybody reported me for having a drink. Hey! Don't look at me like that. I wasn't knocking back spirits. Just a beer. Well, the police turn up, and there's alcohol in my system, and I'm incarcerated—mandatory three months, for one stupid beer during pregnancy, even as a first offence." Gerard is open-mouthed.

"I didn't tell you about the pregnancy in case you brought in lawyers, judged me unfit."

"I might have done."

"Anyway, I was happy to have a baby. I've no regrets. He's a lovely boy."

"And I want to meet him, but I need to know what you expect from me."

"I don't want to share him, if that's what you're thinking. We have a nice life together. But it's like this: he's smarter than me. He deserves some private tuition, and a few extras—better tech, better clothes. And later, a few helpful connections. You could open doors for him when he's older."

Gerard is sweating. He feels he's getting dragged into Freya's long-term plans. He blurts, "I told my wife about this. She understands, but she's not exactly overjoyed that our son has a half-brother. I can't blame her."

"I'm not interested in your wife—only in Skye."

"That's fine, then. My wife wants me to make a deal with you. A one-time deal. A single payment. You'll have to sign papers."

"You've not even met him yet."

"Which is better. Let's talk about the money first, the compensation."

She walks off to the back of the deck. He joins her, and they look out over the waterway. Each seems hesitant to make the first move, to make the first indication of a ballpark figure. It's all about trade, Gerard reckons—this much effort, this much risk, for this much reward. He imagines times past, the dock jammed with ships, under repair after long sea journeys. Iron pots to Africa, slaves to the New World, sugar to Bristol.

"You know, Gerard. That was the best summer—when we met."

※

Half an hour later, Freya collects Skye and brings him aboard. Gerard sees a blur as the boy jumps off the gangway. He's a strong-looking lad, and Gerard admits to himself that he expected a skinny kid, a waif—runt of the litter. He looks like a boy who spends most of his time outdoors. A surfer boy. Freya walks away towards the prow, and the boy jogs along the flat open deck. He stops to lean over the side of boat, gripping the iron rails. And then he jumps, trying to grab hold of the iron rigging. Freya is smart after all; this detour around the deck gives Gerard time to look at the boy so that by the time they approach him, with Gerard's heart quickening, he has already assimilated quite a deal about this eleven-year-old.

He's robust and assured in his movements. Gerard can tell without any exchange of words that he's a boy at ease with himself. And as they come close, side by side, he sees Freya's features echoed in the boy—her hair, her good bone structure. But Gerard wonders if the boy's open smile betrays him, a hint of some hidden incapacity. The shame of this thought makes his face burn.

Freya says, "Skye, tell my friend Gerard what you just told me."

"I said, let's you and me sail a ship one day." His voice has the same lilt as his mother's.

She says, "And you'd have an important job, wouldn't you, Skye? Tell Gerard."

"I'd climb the rigging. I'd be the lookout." He looks across the waterway, his hand to his forehead. "Land ahoy!"

⚹

He wanted them to stay longer. Despite that, when they waved from the gangway he felt relief mainly. He leans on the railing. The physical aftereffect of the encounter is a tingling in his arms and legs, as though a dog had bared its teeth at him.

He doesn't find Freya attractive. And he's relieved about that. Seeing her for the second time in his life, in daylight this time, the age difference between them was stark. But the boy's going to be a charmer, maybe more so than his own boy.

Louis Conlan-Rossi and Skye Liddicoat—their names clash. He shakes his head; he can't grasp it—he has two sons. That's the thunderbolt. Skye has lived in the world for these past eleven years, and Gerard has shared one half-hour with him. In those eleven years, Gerard has relocated three times, married, won his promotions, taken holidays to France, Italy, South Africa, New York. Travelled all over the world, in fact, like the lucky bastard he is. And the boy has probably never travelled outside England. He's within spitting distance of manhood. He's managed just fine without a father.

⚹

Back home, he refers only once to Freya by name. He says *she* was much older than he expected. He makes that point straight away to Scarlett. "I must have been drunk that night, or the lighting was spectacularly kind."

"Or you were desperate," she says teasing. "Anyway, as long as the boy's happy and well cared for, that's the main thing. Don't feel you have to wade in there and reorganize their lives. I know what you're like. Don't go raising her hopes."

"I said we'll pay compensation for past expenses, and pay a lump sum for his upkeep until he's eighteen. It's up to them how they spend it. I don't think she's the type to keep coming back for more."

"Does she want you and the boy to keep in contact?"

"She didn't say. Should I? He seems a nice enough lad."

"Don't get me involved in—"

"Of course not. But, one day, I think Louis should meet his half-brother. It might expand his understanding. You know?"

His wife frowns and raises one eyebrow in warning: Let's be realistic. She says, "I'll make some tea."

Louis is playing on the floor with his litter of virtual kittens. He likes to tint his kittens in rainbow colours. They clamber on top of him, lick his face, fall off, clamber up again, lick the downy hair on his arms. And all the while, Louis strokes and snuggles each kitten in turn. Compared to Skye, he looks such a baby. He's a quiet kid; it's easy to forget he's in the house. And he's so self-contained, with his kittens and his games.

Gerard gets down on the floor with his son and says, "Hey, I've got an idea, Louis. Let's go to the park tomorrow, have some running races. I'll give you a head start. We could build a den under that monkey tree."

Louis looks up momentarily. His face is a blank, as though his mind is still in an imaginary world with his kittens. Gerard tries again. "I'll put you on my shoulders. You can climb onto the branch of a big tree." Gerard smiles and nods his head. "Well?"

Louis focuses at last and says, "No thanks, Dad."

ALWAYS MIMMY

April

My first ever bequest, and I'm dizzy with indecision. Whatever I buy, it ought to be something rarefied, with heirloom credentials. Among the many possibilities, I'm considering a pendant with an inscription: *In memory of Millie Dack.* Or, less formally: *In my thoughts. Mimmy.* Yesterday, I scanned through all my wish lists in desperation, but every item seemed utterly inconsequential. For the sake of my children—*if* I ever have any, which is looking increasingly unlikely—I'm searching for a memento that will fit my own narrative of my adorable grandmother.

I tug open the door to my flat and make my way to the elevator. Funny how names stick. As a child, I guess I became confused over the two omnipresent women in my life. Obviously, I'd no confusion over my mummy, even though my daddy called her Simone. But the woman my daddy called Mum and my mummy called Millie . . . I don't think I grasped the concept of a grandmother. Millie became Mimmy in my little head. So I grew up with a mummy and a Mimmy. Later on, and unlike my school friends, I didn't ever say nana or granny or grandma. Always Mimmy.

Waiting for the elevator. The safe choice is definitely a designer necklace or brooch. But jewellery is so easily lost. Better to buy an item that never leaves the flat. A rare print—the same artist, or same era, as the print Mimmy gave me for my twenty-first birthday. Not a bad idea. The pairing would be a talking point, an embellishment of the original gift and possibly the start of an even longer narrative.

Mimmy's birthday present was a print by Alfred Wallis, an unschooled artist who turned out naive seascapes, harbour scenes and the like in Cornwall. Mimmy held a fascination with the sea, and not in a soppy, I-love-watching-the-waves kind of way. She worked for many years in the Department of World Trade, shepherding ministerial delegations and such like. Not surprisingly, she became interested in the history of sea trade, trading routes and pirates. So at odds with Mimmy's character, it seemed to me growing up, because Mimmy never travelled beyond British shores once she retired.

I tut at my side-on reflection in the hallway mirrors. Awful posture. I stretch myself upright, adding a couple of inches to my height. But it's an effort to maintain. I feel jaded, as though I slept for only five minutes last night. My brain no doubt was processing the heirloom possibilities from the moment I closed my eyes.

My first thought when I woke: Be sensible, pay down your debts. However, that resolution faded during my shower. I returned to the bedroom and set out the clothes suggested by my virtual assistant, Polly, based on the day's schedule of appointments and social engagements. I dressed at speed—I was heading out for my early meeting with the breakfast club—twirled around and grabbed an arm clasp from the glass jewellery tray on my chest of drawers. And I froze. Inspiration at last. I stared at the glittering crystal Victoriana—two glass trinket pots, a ring holder and two glass candlesticks. I'd spend my inheritance on something similarly elegant and personal, which I'd see every day.

For me, the jewellery tray and its crystal pots hark back to a time when people had fewer possessions, and those possessions were chosen after lengthy deliberation. My great-great-great-great aunt—or great-great-great-great-great aunt—was the original owner of the tray set. It might have been a wedding present, I never did know, but I'm sure it was a highly prized possession. No doubt, unlike me, my aunt kept the glassware free of dust and beautifully arranged. My face flushes. I imagine my aunt's tray arranged with a dainty watch in one lidded glass pot, two bracelets in the other, an eternity ring and an engagement ring on the ring holder, three sets of earrings neatly placed in the tray. She'd be shocked to see it now. I've stuffed the pots with tat from my teenage years—the glass lids are perched atop. And between the pots, I've piled all my day-to-day jewellery.

I step into the elevator, raise my left hand to my face and speak to the tip of my forefinger: "Draw up a shortlist of commemorative purchases, Polly, to remind me of Mimmy." The choice will probably come down to jewellery, a seascape or a luxury holiday. But Polly may come up with a better idea. I can't help but smile as the elevator descends. I should buy an armchair—that's how I see Mimmy in my mind's eye. Mimmy was a nest-builder by nature, a contented armchair voyager of the high seas.

Polly, her voice inside my head, asks, "Is this shortlist my priority?"

"Absolutely." I button up my sculpted jacket. "Polly, why did you suggest this get-up for today? There's nothing special in the calendar; no presentations."

"In line with your aspirations for 2120, Julia, I've requested a revised search for a romantic interest from your new agency. You ought to maintain a permanent state of preparedness. I've now requested one hundred per cent similar."

"Ha! One hundred per cent *different* was a total disaster. Swinging the pendulum won't solve anything."

X

A circular table for eight, white starched table linen, at the Connaught Hotel in Mayfair—the best buffet breakfast this side of London, and a convenient location for the six of us regular attendees who live west of the centre. We'll all commute to the Square Mile of the financial district when I guillotine our discussion at seven o'clock. I'm proud we've kept going with these meetings—the second Tuesday of every month—and as I instigated the idea, I try always to arrive a few minutes before six. It's important we meet as early as possible in the day, before our rational selves have fully emerged from sleep. The others indulge me in this, but I'm convinced I'm right on this one. Ideally, we should roll out of bed and hold a holo-meeting, but all things considered, we prefer to meet in person without home distractions.

The core of our breakfast group includes me, of course, and four other members who studied at the Saïd Business School in Oxford. Over the past five years, we've increased our number to form an informal think tank—and that's a bit overblown, I suppose. Let's call it a discussion group. Anyway, the fact is we get together to rekindle the level of debate in our Saïd seminars. It's worth the effort to keep in regular contact with people who are the smartest of the smart in central and investment banking, sales and trading, private equity. Mostly, it's a brilliant shortcut, keeping each of us abreast of a wide field, gaining rich insight from people who read more than the quality press. People who drill down.

By four minutes past six, everyone has arrived, and Javid—always the last—rushes straight up to me at the buffet; these central bank people aren't early starters. "I thought you'd have begun without me, Julia." He grabs pastries and fruit. "That'll do for me."

Should I tell him? "You've got sleep in your eyes, Javid."

"Oh, thanks for . . . Sorry." He pokes around in the corner of his eyes. "Shit! You're right. What a mess." Got to laugh.

He places his order with the waiter for green tea as Chantelle, this year's chair, says, "If we all have our plates piled high and drinks ordered, let's make a start. Labour markets! For the coming three months, we'll discuss a persistently thorny issue—the participation of lower-skilled citizens in the workforce. Specifically, we'll address ourselves to the question: What are the obstacles, political and educational, in creating gainful employment for an underskilled underclass? And to start us off, Javid will give a brief spiel, as deliberately provocative as usual, I expect."

As Javid wipes crumbs from his shirt, I receive an emergency alert from Polly—though Polly's understanding of what constitutes an emergency does *not* coincide with mine. I duck down to the side, bring my left hand to my face and whisper, "Not now." She'll be calling about the heirloom purchase. She buzzes again. Well, she can buzz as much as she likes.

Javid starts by posing a question. "Isn't there a simple fix here? Why pour government money into benefits for the underemployed"—he looks around the group—"when we can cut subsidies for automation, sack a few droids, sacrifice a bit of productivity, but bring more citizens into the workforce?"

We all shout him down. "That horse has already bolted," I call out.

Javid smiles, raises his palms to the group. "I knew you'd say that. Just testing. But we had to get that argument out of the way."

"A total nonstarter," Chantelle mutters.

I turn aside again—Polly is driving me nuts. "What? Be quick."

"I've found a perfect match, Julia! He's in London until this evening. There's no other overlap in your calendars for the next five weeks. You must meet him for lunch. I've set things up with his personal assistant. I'll send you—"

"Okay. Now, *desist*."

✕

"Do you ever feel you're not in charge of your life?" he says as a greeting. His name is Richard, he's a management consultant, and that's all the information I've had time to read. I hoped he'd be late so I could scan the essentials. Sadly, he was prompt.

"Like today? A pile of work, and I'm suddenly instructed I have a date. And it won't wait."

"Exactly," he says. We shake hands. Neither of us seems willing to release contact.

I'll suspend judgement on his little-boy haircut. After all, according to Polly, the data match is categorical, almost irresistible. And I hope Richard heard the same from his assistant. He's my kind of fella, looks-wise, so I've nailed *that* in the screening process, though he's slightly taller than my stated preference. I don't like looking up at a man, gets bloody uncomfortable.

"I'm sorry I passed on your restaurant suggestion, Richard. I had a big breakfast thing. Just not hungry."

"This is perfect." We're at the thirty-second floor of the Walkie Talkie building, in the arboretum. "Or is this your usual venue for a date?" He laughs. After a moment's hesitation, I decide not to take offence.

"You're being cheeky already," I say, adding, "If you must know, I tend to meet my girlfriends here before a big night out. Gives me a buzz."

In fact, Richard guessed correctly. This *is* my default place for a first date. It's in the heart of the city, therefore handy; it's public; and the fabulous view gives both parties plenty to talk about.

I take charge. I lead the way to the full-height windows that over-look the Thames and point down towards the opposite bank of the river to the steel and glass canopy over Hay's Wharf. "See that?" He nods. "Hay's Wharf was once known as the Larder of London. It handled most of the dry goods coming into London in the nineteenth century—all the tea, for example. It later burned down and was rebuilt, and then it was bombed in World War II. It's a tourist attraction these days." We stroll along the window, briefly distracted from assessing one another by the forest of high-rises south of the river. We take a seat in a niche set among yuccas and ferns.

"I don't know about you, Richard, but I haven't had time to read the briefing paper on you."

"Me neither. Let's do a two-minute icebreaker, if that isn't too hackneyed for you. We can do our homework later. Unless you feel I'm a nonstarter."

We cover the bases—where we work, where we've studied, where we've lived. Our assistants know all of this already, and more, and they'd have flagged up any dealbreakers: a major differential in salary or education, any genome alerts. It's so reassuring; leaves me free to concentrate on subtle clues to his character. I like the way he sits— relaxed, no fidgeting—as though he's happy to be in the moment, confident without being overly assertive. I don't try to gauge how I myself come across; gave that up a long time ago. But I do know that if I assume a confident pose, I'm likely to *feel* more confident. Shoulders back.

"How long's your lunch break, Julia?"

"Another fifteen minutes, tops." I grimace in apology. "I didn't want to delay meeting you, but you know how it is. I'm having a crazy day. So help me out." I place my elbow on the back of the seat. "I have a conundrum. I've received a bequest from my grandmother, and I can't decide what to do with it. What's your advice?"

"*That's* a good question."

"It's a real question. It's not a test. I honestly want to know how you'd approach the problem."

"Well, first of all, a bequest cannot be described as a problem, can it?" he says.

"Agreed."

"Unless you feel pressure to spend the money one way rather than another. Is anyone trying to influence you?"

"Not exactly. I'm trying to imagine what my grandmother would like me to do. And I want my father's approval."

"With my professional hat on"—he mimes crowning his head with a hat, which is rather corny, but I have to admit, *on him* it's quite endearing—"I'd say pay down any debt that's running at a high interest rate. But I guess you've a decent salary in your line of work, so this could be an opportunity for fun. Depends how much money is involved. Could it be a gamechanger? Could you buy a romantic cottage in the country? Or a one-off holiday, to a space resort even? To be honest, I think your best bet is jewellery or a collectible."

I shoot back: "I'd stress about losing an expensive piece of jewellery." Seeing his face sag, I add, "But you're definitely right about a collectible. We're on the same wavelength there."

When I take my leave of Richard—and I must say, as first dates go, I can mark Richard as eight out of ten—I decide Polly needs a tailored briefing. "Polly, dear, amend the search criteria for the commemorative purchase, will you? Forget jewellery, if that's the track you're taking. Hone in on collectibles, travel, holidays, adventure."

Ж

I drop into the sofa, my jacket already thrown to the floor. Eyes closed, slow deep breaths. I've yet to read the briefing paper on Richard. Resisted the temptation to do so back at the office and during my commute home. He's by far the most promising date of the three so far with this agency. He deserves careful, quiet consideration, but only after a rest.

When I signed up for the full service, I spent an eight-hour day taking part in psychological assessments, followed by thrice-weekly therapy sessions for two months. All aimed at identifying my personality type and any sensitivities. It's the sensitivities that constitute the make or break in most relationships—or so I was told. I did dither about making such a big time commitment, but as the agency consultant said,

"Why wait a year, two years, to discover you're not suited to someone? We won't let you waste your time like that." I had to get serious about finding a partner, if only to stop my parents worrying.

Although I've had plenty of dates, I haven't had an actual boyfriend for five years—not since finishing with Josh on the eve of my thirtieth birthday. He'd failed to pay his share of the rent on time for the fourth month in succession. I couldn't bear the build-up of tension as the due date approached. It was too much. After that break-up, I promised myself—and I've kept to it—that I'd never date another unreliable type; creative genes are fascinating in friends, but I can't cope with the intimate proximity.

In the shadow of my disappointment with Josh, I'm looking for a man who's at least as solvent as I am. Makes me sound bitchy, but it's plain embarrassing being the one with money, the one constantly saying, "I'll cover that if you like." In fact, I stopped doing that after six months with Josh. I stopped booking dinner dates or concerts. Instead, I found inconspicuous outlets for my spending—luxury body products, weekly manicures, expensive lunch dates with girlfriends. I treated myself with total discretion when I travelled overseas on business trips. A case in point—my tour, last summer, of the French Riviera, a fact-finding visit to assess potential sites for new offshore solar farms. All very interesting in itself, but I timetabled my itinerary so I could dine each evening at a Michelin-starred restaurant.

I drag myself over to the wine cooler, pour a glass of Puligny-Montrachet and take a large gulp. I feel better already. My extravagances are becoming a habit—I accept I should take stock. By now, I should be living in a better part of town. Most of my friends are thinking of bigger homes, having children. And it isn't cheap to conceive these days. Honestly, you need to earn a pile of money just to be poor in this city.

I *should* use Mimmy's bequest to pay down some debt—make a fresh start, fewer fripperies. And as for buying a memento of Mimmy, I won't go overboard.

I open the briefing paper on Richard and skip through the exposition on education, family, genome and employment. Reaching the section titled "Personality Traits," I feel my stomach rumble. Pure nerves. Braced for disappointment. I pick out the descriptives. Nothing too unusual—*personable, loyal, magnanimous.* The challenge is to spot the slightest hint of a negative trait. In Richard's case, I notice one possibility; the report says he *tends to be indulgent.* That can be a good thing. Depends on who exactly he's being indulgent towards. And indulgent with what? Attention, sympathy, money?

I run my index finger around the top of my glass, take another slug of wine. Do I match Richard? With Josh, I showed my natural generosity until it all went too far. I'm certainly not tight with money. And I'm attentive to Mum and Dad.

I skip forward to the section titled "Sensitivities." It seems that Richard does not take compliments at face value. He didn't receive sufficient praise as he developed towards adulthood. He's suspicious of praise, yet he still craves it. I can handle that; my parents lavished praise on me, and I'm happy to dish it out too. In fact, I love praising people—friends, colleagues. No hardship there.

Richard must decide for himself if he can cope with *my* personality traits—specifically, my tendency towards impulsivity. Not to mention my sensitivity arising, so I'm *told*, from my solo conception—that I'm apt to form intense friendships with other women. The shrink suggested that I'm deeply affected by my lack of genetic diversity. Where's the logic in that? These people do talk utter bollocks at times. I'm emotionally well connected to Simone, my "mum," possibly more so than I am to my dad, because although I love him, he can be bolshie; tries to press his opinions on everyone.

The shrink, I reckon, latched on to a single remark: I said I wouldn't choose a solo conception if it was avoidable—I'd prefer to splice my genes with a sexual partner as part of a long-term relationship. And *that* was my dad talking, to be honest.

Richard will have finished his homework on *me* by now. It does speed up the whole process, but there's scope for obfuscation. The process can't detect sins of omission. For one thing, I didn't mention my love of fine dining when asked about my interests. Though I did say I'd take one glass of good wine *any day* to three glasses of plonk.

When I'm ready to commit to someone—and Richard could be the one—then I'll be obliged to reveal the past three months' bank statements and global assets. If I delay reaching that commitment stage, I can rein in my spending so the statements appear chaste. He'll no doubt do some budgetary housekeeping himself. And if we stay with the programme and decide to marry, there's a compulsory "come clean" session in which we're coaxed by a life coach to bring everything to the table. Thumbscrews, in other words.

※

"Polly, call my dad." It's a short walk to Acton Main Line station, past the coffeehouses on Horn Lane. My friends aren't convinced, but I reckon Acton is a nice enough part of London to bring up a family. And it's not too far from my parents. They've asked me over for lunch on Saturday, so I'd like to buy a Mimmy memento before then. Ideally, I'll take it with me, together with a bottle of champagne. What's taking Dad so long to answer?

"Hi Julia. You're not cancelling Saturday, are you?" His voice is deeper than I expected.

"Sorry, were you asleep?"

"Not really. Just coming round."

"I want your opinion if you're awake enough, Dad. I'm thinking of buying an antique globe—a small one to sit on my oak sideboard, like a centrepiece. I thought it would be a lovely reminder of Mimmy. You know, telling all her stories about pirates." I don't mention that the globe was Polly's top suggestion.

"That's a great idea. Go for it. But why an antique?"

"Well, it's like an investment, makes it more precious. And, I'd like the oceans as they were in pirate days—with the Maldives, and *all* the Solomon Islands."

"Could be expensive."

"You'd be surprised. They must have made globes by the thousand. I thought I'd use the rest"—I look around to check that no one is in hearing distance—"the rest of the money to pay down some of my mortgage."

"Bloody hell, Julia. That's woken me up. When did *you* become so sensible? Wait 'til I tell . . . Hey, Simone, wake up and hear—"

"Very funny, Dad. Anyway, I'm nearly at the station, and I've some work to do en route. I'll see you Saturday. Love to Mum."

That's *that* sorted out. I reckon Richard will admire my choice of memento, once he understands the pirate connection. Let's hope we'll meet again; after all, we've so much going for us.

At the station entrance, I give the command: "Polly, sweetie. Buy the globe."

THEY'RE ALL THINKING THE SAME

Theo Munroe-Steane lies on his duvet in the bathtub, takes a sliver of soap from the tiled nook and throws it at the mirror above the sink. The sliver sticks for two seconds, then drops. Satisfaction level: nonexistent. The white smudge on the mirror mocks him for his timidity; he didn't have the guts to throw the full, as-yet-unwetted bar of soap.

Downstairs, Theo's father, Nathen, clears the breakfast dishes. He looks over his shoulder and says, "Fancy getting a baby-sitter tonight?"

Theo's mother, Amelie, is checking the weather forecast before her Saturday morning run. "Er, could do. We've no other plans this weekend, have we?"

"None. Or we could take the boys out for an early dinner," says Nathen.

"Either way."

Theo is now forty-three minutes into his lock-in, and he has a crick in his neck. Neither of his parents, he suspects, is aware of his self-imposed solitary confinement. He should have brought his pillows and more than one game. The bathroom isn't ideal for battle scenarios, it's too low and rectangular, but it's fine for Scuba Diver. He decides he might as well tiptoe across the landing to fetch the pillows—then restart his confinement. And while he's in his bedroom, he'll search for chocolates and snacks under his bed.

He places his forearms on either side of the bath and pushes himself up, slipping a little as the duvet shifts on the bath's smooth azure surface. With one foot on the bathroom floor, he freezes. Footsteps on the stairs. He can tell from the weight and speed that his mum is on her way up. She turns the doorknob.

"Who's . . . ? That you, Theo?"

"I'm not coming out until you cancel the haircut. You can't make me." His mum doesn't reply. Theo knows he's caught her off-guard. He has the early advantage, which he rams home: "It's a free world, if you hadn't noticed."

His mum mentioned over breakfast that she'd booked a barber's appointment for both him and his brother, Seb, next weekend. "Have a think about a new hairstyle, Theo. Now you're getting older you could try something shorter—like Seb's?" Theo replied that he liked his hair long. That should have ended the discussion, to his mind, but she said, "I think you'd look really handsome with short hair." His dad chipped in, "You'd take less time in the shower too." It was a pincer movement; it made him suspicious. Had they rehearsed? He stood up from the breakfast table and said, "I like my hair long, so you can cancel the haircut." They carried on reading. He left his toast and marmalade unfinished, walked upstairs. They probably didn't even register that he'd spoken.

He should have slammed the door and stomped up the stairs. In the future, he'll make more noise, act like his older brother. He needs to observe his brother and learn. Seb can sense the precise location of an invisible threshold—the line he must cross to provoke a parental reaction. He deploys one of two tactics: he hikes the volume or he swears. And he knows exactly how far he can go.

His mum clears her throat. "Come on, Theo, unlock the door. If you *must* know, the haircut wasn't my idea in the first place. Gr'Atticus put the thought in my head. He's coming over with Nan Toni at the weekend, and I thought it would be a nice surprise if you had a new hairstyle. You know, before they set off on their big trip."

"What's my hair got to do with their trip? That's totally illogical." He's still too measured. He closes his eyes and imagines he is Seb. He says, "I'm not taking style notes from someone who's over a hundred years old," and increases the decibels: "It's fucking ridiculous."

Silence all round. He's relieved his mum can't see his blushes.

In a lowered voice, she says, "Gr'Atticus would be so upset if he heard you say that, Theo."

He steels himself, "What do you take me for? Obviously, I wouldn't say it to his face."

"He wasn't offering fashion advice. He made a perfectly innocent remark, that you'd look a lot older if you had shorter hair."

"You've all been talking about me behind my back, haven't you? You're not respecting me."

His mum mutters; he can't hear her. Then, clearly and slowly, she says, "We know how smart you are, Theo. We've always respected you. But you shouldn't be swearing at me. I wouldn't let Seb get away with that."

"I'm not coming out."

And with that she walks downstairs. Theo climbs back in the bath. His mum has outmanoeuvred him. Even if she relents on the haircut, she's got him cornered for swearing. He's such an amateur. Seb told him so last week. Their dad had asked who'd left the milk out of the fridge overnight. Theo admitted he'd done it. Afterwards, Seb took him aside and said, "You didn't need to own up. He'd never know for sure who did it. He knows Mum might have left it out and forgotten. Just keep your mouth shut and look innocent—should be easy enough for you." Seb *does* look out for him.

⋊⋉

Theo's stomach rumbles. He didn't finish his breakfast, and he has zero food supplies. Seb wouldn't make such an elementary error. He climbs out of the bath, leans over the sink and drinks water straight from the tap. He hears heavy, steady footsteps. It must be his dad, because Seb is out at football practice, and in any case, Seb runs two steps at a time up the stairs.

There's a knock. "Theo? I told Seb I'd watch the second half of his footy match. Fancy coming along?" His dad must surely know about the argument, but he sounds perfectly normal. "Seb would love to see you on the touchline. Fact is, your mum's going for a run. I can't leave you home alone."

"I'm not coming out if you're going to talk about haircuts. You can't make me have one."

"But we'd like to talk about it without escalating to DEFCON Two. And, you'll have to apologize to your mother for swearing at her."

This is probably the moment to back down, but Theo imagines Seb nudging him forward. "She started it."

Another silence. And then, "Please yourself. You can explain to Seb why neither of us turned up to watch him play."

⋊⋉

Amelie is waiting in her running gear at the foot of the stairs. She says, "He must be starving, Nathen. What shall we do?"

"Go for your run. I'll put a plate of food in his bedroom and tell him he's made his point."

"Good idea. He'll be nervous about coming downstairs to face us. I'm sure he'll apologize later on." She puts her hands on her hips and sighs. "I was looking forward to a noneventful weekend."

As she leaves the house, she slams the front door. Over winter the door swelled, and it's still sticking, even though the tulips are out. She sets off on her usual run through the back streets towards Burgess Park, makes her usual detour to pick up the original straight route of the Grand Surrey Canal, filled in to make roads nearly two hundred years ago. It's a one-hour route if she makes two circuits of the park. She'd intended to try a new route today, but she feels too distracted by Theo. She just hopes the run is long enough to clear her head, shed some guilt.

She feels absolutely rotten she brought Gr'Atticus into the argument, but it's a measure of her desperation. If only Theo would cooperate, cut his mop of hair, she might start to relax. They'd look like a family instead of the hotchpotch revealed in Theo's birthday photographs. Ten years old last month, and the family photograph—everyone gathered around the birthday cake—screamed that Theo was the odd one out. If he'd wear his hair shorter, the difference would be tempered.

A couple of years ago she could have dropped Theo off at the barber's and said, "Time for a big-boy's haircut." Stupidly, she's left it far too late. So, when Atticus commented that Theo's long wavy hair made him look young, he unwittingly supplied Amelie with a ploy for broaching the subject. And Theo adores his great-grandfather. She reaches the park entrance. Small kids and their parents block the path. She slows down and dodges her way past.

Everyone in the family keeps quiet, but they're all thinking the same thing—she speeds up—Theo doesn't fit in. He's taller, slimmer, blonder. And Amelie suspects he'll be much, much smarter.

X

Theo breaks into a sweat when the front door slams—a motherly meltdown. He wracks his memory, can't recall a single moment when his mum ever lost her temper with him. He's seen her fly off the handle with Seb.

He wallows in his dry bath. He does the slightest thing wrong and his mum goes catatonic, as though he's expected at all times to be perfect. He's a fool. There's no point in staging this lock-in—Seb will laugh at him when he gets home. There's a bathroom downstairs. No one is inconvenienced but himself.

None of them know why he's so pissed off, and he's not going to spell it out. Seb would crack a joke, and his parents would do that *thing* he hates. Whenever he shows interest in a new hobby, they chase around, massively agitated, looking for special classes and extra tuition. He hasn't told them he's been writing poetry over the past six months. He's doing it on the quiet. Well, not exactly on the quiet, because he leaves his games on autoplay so they'll think he's still fixated on that particular time sink.

The fact is, he can see his future unfolding before him, and he's been reading the biographies of famous poets to check their childhood achievements. He's not doing badly in comparison. He's going to be a serious poet one day, and more to the point, he doesn't see himself as a short-haired poet. If he gives in to his parents, he'll have to wait until he's eighteen to start growing his hair again. And that will take at least two years, probably three. He'll be twenty-one before he looks like himself again, and his best work might already be behind him.

Perhaps he should negotiate a peace settlement via his dad; his dad won't make a big deal of it, whereas his mum will want to reason with him, talk him into submission. He doesn't mind saying he's sorry. He wants to. And he'd like to end it all before Seb comes home. He climbs out of the bath again, listens at the door. He could slip out, go to his room and act as though nothing happened. But he doesn't want his dad to catch him coming out—he'd have to admit defeat.

And coming full circle—if he ends the lock-in without some recognition of his rights, his parents might never respect him again. He climbs back into the bath.

X

Nathen prepares a plate of cheese, pickle and bread, and brews a mug of tea. He places them on a tray, adds a chocolate bar, then removes it— "Don't be such a pushover," he mumbles—and walks across the hallway to the bottom of the stairs. He hears the sound effects of an underwater fight coming from the bathroom. He clenches his teeth. Some blasted genius. He's gaming again as though nothing happened, oblivious to the upset he's causing at the start of what should have been a relaxing weekend with no commitments. And Amelie has enough stress at the moment. Nathen always thought she had the ideal job, conserving paintings in the back rooms of the museum—quiet, meditative work. But now that she's won promotion she's handling a few managerial tasks, dealing with interference from patrons. She came home exasperated yesterday. The worst of the patrons were insistent on turning back the clock—refusing to accept that paintings *do* age, and should be allowed to.

X

Amelie starts her second circuit of the park. There's a tightness in her calves, so she can't settle into a rhythm; she hasn't stretched as much as she should between runs. She wonders if Nathen has talked Theo out of the bathroom. If *anyone* can defuse the crisis, it's Nathen. So calm. He works in human resources, has defused worse situations. She can't help thinking that their lives would be incredibly straightforward if they'd stopped at one. She'd convinced herself that she needed a second child to feel like a proper family.

First time around, she wanted a natural pregnancy, which Nathen supported. She had assumed she'd do the same for her second pregnancy. But at the age of two and a half, Seb still spoke in single words— no two-word phrases. She and Nathen were anxious he might have developmental problems, so they decided on remote gestation for the second baby. Even though all their relatives told them not to worry about Seb's speech, that every child was different, the clinicians preyed on their guilty feelings. Why take the risk of having two children with learning difficulties?

She and Nathen paid for the standard germ line modifications to delete the mutation load, and allowed the clinic to screen for the most vital embryo. Then—going too far—they paid for aesthetic tweaks. What were they thinking? Two intelligent adults who allowed themselves to be bamboozled.

Before Theo reached full term in the gestation clinic, Seb discovered his powers of speech. He'd skipped the *ba-ba-ba-ba* baby phase; his first utterance was a complete sentence. He finished eating his lunch— mashed potato and flaked fish, she'll never forget—licked the bottom of his dish and spoke, plain as day: "That was good, Mummy." At the time, she thought, Now he tells me! If he'd said that six months ago, we'd have saved a ton of money.

Nevertheless, she and Nathen were on a high when they collected Theo from the gestation unit. They felt life would be replete with possibility for this child. He would simply reach out and achieve greatness. And, as anticipated, Theo hit all the developmental milestones early—early to roll from his back to his front, early to sit up unaided, early to say his first word. However, when Amelie inspected the photos of Theo's tenth birthday party, she realized—apart from baulking at his mop of hair—that his persistent cherubic looks were overstated, at odds somehow with his intelligence. With that realization, Amelie suffered a panic attack, which she passed off as work stress. Since then, she has entertained a troubling thought—that she came away from the gestation unit with someone else's baby.

Since the panic attack, she's suffered a recurring nightmare. She dreams she's swimming in the sea with Theo as a baby. It's lovely for a while, but then she deliberately lets go of Theo; she allows him to drift away.

There's no mistaking that Seb is hers, theirs. He's a great kid—a bit cheeky. Probably gets that particular trait from her side of the family. But he'll need a bit of cheek, a bit of charm, to get on in life. He doesn't have Theo's advantages.

A runner crosses her path. They recognize one another and they nod. Neither of them musters a smile. She wonders if he harbours equally dark thoughts during his run in the park.

Hitting race pace along the straight path bisecting Burgess Park, Amelie almost outruns her worst self-accusation: she should have listened to Nathen. He'd suggested they keep things simple with Theo's conception, but he gave way in the face of her own certainty. Is it an only-child thing—does she overstate her desires, her wants?

She pulls up short, sits down at a bench, head in hands. Get over it, she tells herself. Accept Theo as he is. She wipes away her tears and pretends for the sake of a passing runner that she's checking her stats. Cramp is coming on, so she stands and stretches.

𝕏

Nathen pauses by the bathroom door. "I'm putting your lunch in your bedroom." There's no reply. He crosses the landing, pushes open the bedroom door and clears a space on Theo's detritus-strewn desk—a tangle of printed doodles, half-finished constructions, wearables, a sound-effects bracelet prised open. It seems counterintuitive to Nathen that Theo's room favours a bomb site, whereas Seb's room is more ordered. The explanation could be that Theo's mind is in constant flux, and as a result, he shifts restlessly from one activity to another, and to another.

He pushes a hand through his hair and sighs. Theo might never settle on one thing; he doesn't seem to have Seb's tenacity. Seb has two passions, which haven't changed over the past three or four years.

Namely, football and drawing. He's capable of real focus. And though Seb's room is untidy at the weekend with strewn football kit, all his art materials—pens, pencils, sketchbooks, tablets, coloured papers—are always carefully set out on his desk and shelves.

Nan Toni got him started. She says he showed interest in Dominic's studio. In fact, Nathen reckons Seb, as a small child, was purely interested in the studio door's bolts and padlocks. Whatever the truth, Nan Toni set up a child's desk in the studio and gave Seb free rein with old brushes and paints, scraps of paper and crayons. Theo never developed the same curiosity for the studio.

Nathen sits in Theo's revolving chair, puts his feet up on the bed. He knows, in time, the differences between his sons will make more sense. He keeps his expectations in check when it comes to Seb. He praises him when the occasion arises. This week, at the midweek match, he praised Seb for an unselfish pass in front of the goal mouth. And he's impressed that when Seb's friends come over to hang out, he allows Theo to join them. Nathen can't imagine the boys will stay close as they get older, but it's pleasing that Seb looks out for his brother. And Theo looks up to Seb, which is touching.

If he and Amelie were to have a third child, he'd insist on clinic gestation. He didn't like seeing her pregnant. Turned his stomach. Embarrassing at times too; people assumed they'd hit hard times.

Nathen takes a piece of cheese from the plate. He's about to take a bite when there's a creak of floorboards. Theo stands in the doorway with his arms around his duvet. He says, "Sorry, Dad."

"Good. Can we start the day again, please?"

Theo smiles, and Nathen says, "And, seriously, I think you should *at least* have a trim. Get your hair off your shoulders."

"I don't trust the barber. He'll cut too much off."

"*I'll* give you a trim. Let's do it before your mother gets home."

MR. FILIPKOWSKI'S LIBRARY

At the end of her shift, Freya Liddicoat strides out onto the Cornish coastal path from the headland restaurant and, despite her neck ache, performs mental maths on her tipping stats. Five tables: a 20 tip on a bill of 180; 90 on 410; 20 on 290 (no smile for them next time); 100 on 320 (that totally made her day); zero on 95 (the kitchen's fault, serving up *cold* steamed mussels). So that's . . . ? She adds the tips. Two hundred and thirty. And adds the bills. Twelve ninety-five. Overall she can't complain. The basic pay is the best she's had in a restaurant, and she keeps her own tips. She'd make more if she worked the evening shifts, but on this side of town, the posh side, most customers order a three-course lunch with wine, and tip accordingly. She lifts her palm to her mouth and says, "Two hundred and thirty as a percentage of twelve hundred and ninety-five." She knows she's shy of 20 per cent, but she wants the precise figure.

The number *17.76%* flashes on her wristband.

Not bad. Way short of her record breaker: Valentine's Day 2119—a vermilion sunset on cue—at 26 per cent. Share the love! No one wants to look stingy when pursuing a new love interest. Inevitably, there's a downside—tips are abysmal the weekend after Valentine's.

Even on the best days, one table will drag you down, each time for a different reason. A bit like *Anna Karenina*, as she once explained to Skye. Happy diners are generically happy; unhappy diners are specific in their misery: a delay in being seated, delays in service, cold food that should be hot (as per today), wine arriving halfway through the starters, diners feeling hurried through their courses, no Chilean sodding chardonnay. But Freya tries to keep bitter feelings under wraps. Any angst she *does* feel, she unloads among friends; many are servers themselves. They turn the misery around, have a laugh. Anyway, there's no point getting down, because as she keeps telling herself, waiting tables has served her well; one of the few jobs that droids can't handle.

Skye always asks her over their evening meal, "Any big tippers today, Mum?" This evening she'll tell him she served three sets of twins at lunchtime, all sat together at one table. It isn't true, but he falls for her stories every time: "Honestly? Really?" That's one of the advantages of this walking commute—along the headland, around Fistral Bay and around the golf course—it gives her time to make up a story. It's a bit of fun. She wants to make him laugh, help him to feel positive. And as well as the stories, she brings home her restaurant skills. Even if they're eating egg on toast, she sets the table properly, the cutlery neatly ordered—the blade of the knife facing inwards—Verdicchio bottle as a water carafe, and a napkin each; she has an impressive collection of purloined table linen.

There's a northwesterly breeze, and though it chills her back, she's glad of the wind assist on the two-mile walk into town. She checks the time. She should make the three o'clock bus from Newquay heading north. Some of the restaurant staff take a taxi into town, but she can't splash out like that. She's done the sums; she saves enough money walking between town and the restaurant to buy a decent birthday and Christmas present for Skye. Two good presents a year, and a mother who works hard, plus funny stories about the customers. He'll remember all that, she hopes, rather than the shabby state of their accommodation.

As she reaches the highest point on the headland path, a skylark shoots vertically from the grassland by her feet. She startles, then stops and peers, trying to spot the skylark's nest. Nature can be dumb. Why would mother skylark build a nest so close to the path? A dog could easily trample the nest and smash the eggs. She looks up and ahead; there's an elderly man walking a dog—looks like a springer spaniel.

When she quits this job—*if* she quits it—she'll miss this daily walk on dry days. And who wouldn't? There can't be a better walk to work anywhere in England. The Atlantic Ocean crashing into Fistral Bay and, on the other side of the headland, Crantock Beach and the tidal stretch of the Gannel River. The palatial houses perched above the Gannel are the second or even third homes of London types. The owners are an inspiration for Freya. They're seriously rich.

The two guys who gave the big tip this lunchtime—100 on a bill of 320—are a case in point. She offered them menus, but they waved them away. The younger man said, "Steak rare for both, a selection of side orders, water, no wine. Thank you." That was all. Menus are for little people, she guesses. She gave them the extra-special treatment, the fine-dining as opposed to the top-bistro service. If ever she becomes rich herself, she'll order off-menu too.

For the past three winters, she and Skye have been house-sitters at five mansions along the Gannel. They live in each house for a week at a time in rotation, and make daily rounds of all five. Blissful in some ways—all-day warmth, so much space in these homes that she and Skye *lose* one another, top-end music and cinema systems, plenty to read. Her favourite house is old Mr. Filipkowski's, with the real library.

It struck Freya, during that first winter, that Mr. Filipkowski had the biggest house she'd ever entered, and it surely couldn't be a coincidence that he owned every book, it seemed, ever written by a business guru, with catchy titles like *My Blunder: 50 Successful Entrepreneurs Reveal Their Worst Decisions*, *Secrets of a Reluctant Billionaire*, *How to Build an Empire on $10*. Freya likes to read his books while sitting in the armchair in his picture window, which overlooks the river. She prefers the river view to the ocean because it's peaceful and colourful at low tide—a gorgeous combination of blue-green pools and the river bed's rippled, orange-y sand.

It's a comedown at the end of winter when they move back to their paint-peeled chalet on the campsite. She's nonetheless grateful; it's a peppercorn rent, and in return she cleans the site's shower block at the start and end of each day. When she and Skye returned after their first winter's house-sitting, she asked Skye—he was seven years old at the time—which house-sit he liked the best. He compared the gardens rather than the houses' interiors, and chose the one with constructed terraces reaching down to the shoreline. The harsh lines of these terraces were softened by ferns and palm trees, and on the second-lowest terrace stood a timber and glass garden house with a sedum roof. Freya wasn't sure how the owner used this room—as a studio or a daytime hangout? Skye paced both sides, declared it was bigger than their own home. And, as though the main house overwhelmed him, he preferred to sleep in the garden house.

Last autumn, the owners of that particular house decided to sell up. Freya cast around to find some way of cheering up her son; he sulked for a full forty-eight hours on hearing the news. So she awarded herself an end-of-employment bonus—that's how she rationalized her decision, because she doubted she'd actually receive a bonus. She removed a guitar from its stand in the living room and hid it among the ferns on the lowest terrace. She'd had a strum on the guitar in the past. Completely untuned. The whole guitar-on-a-stand thing had probably been the idea of an interior designer—icon of Cornish hip. Freya retrieved the guitar from the ferns as soon as the removal van pulled out of the drive.

She told Skye the guitar came from the house, but she didn't say she stole it. She said the owner encouraged her to take something as a thank you. Skye asked if the guitar counted as his birthday present, but Freya said, "No, it's an extra, for putting up with me."

Ж

Freya reaches the high street, sees the three o'clock bus climbing the hill out of Newquay. She groans. It departed three minutes early. She messages Skye: *Back in 45 minutes. 3 o'clock left early again. So annoying.*

She never walks this part of the commute; it's too far, and too steep. She decides to grab a peaceful half-hour and makes her way from the high street downhill towards the clifftop overlooking the town beach. Are things unravelling? It's three and a half weeks since she met Gerard Rossi; he still hasn't transferred any compensation money. And she's missed the bus. *And* she doesn't have much food at home for dinner. Christ on a bike. Get a grip. She's only missed the stupid bus, and with four eggs and a handful of mushrooms, she can make omelettes.

At the clifftop, she flops onto a bench. It's her first rest in six hours. She stretches out her legs, points with her toes to the horizon, hoping to ease her aching calves and buttocks. Her feet are swollen, as though baked in hot sand. She moves her shoulders through several rotations, forwards and then backwards. Why hasn't she heard from Gerard? Has his wife put the brakes on? They're probably arguing about how much Gerard should pay. Or Gerard himself is having second thoughts. She's desperate to nudge him, but daren't risk it; he might feel hectored. He might back off completely.

From her pocket she pulls out a napkin-wrapped sandwich, which the sous-chef handed to her at the end of lunch shift. He said, "In lieu of the lost tip from table twelve. My mistake." At least he fessed up, though one sandwich doesn't cover the loss. She peels back the top slice of rye to take a peek: salmon gravlax and beetroot. She'll save half for Skye—a healthy snack to keep him going until dinner.

After a couple of mouthfuls, she starts to revive. When Gerard sends the money—she *has* to believe he'll do the right thing—she'll thank him profusely, keep him onside, make him feel good about himself. She learned this touchy-feely stuff in one of Mr. Filipkowski's books, *Everyday Psychology for Entrepreneurs*. Gerard's money—what the books call *seed capital*—will activate her business plan, and with a bit of luck she'll be trading before the high season. According to *How to Build a Business Empire on One Good Idea*, Freya realized, she's already had her One Good Idea.

It came to her years ago, while working in a beach bar where all the staff turned their hands to every job: mixing cocktails, food prep, waiting on tables, mopping floors and, in the low season, revarnishing the tables. Hard work, average basic rate, negligible tips. The kitchen had an old hotplate for making pancakes, and she always volunteered for the pancake orders. It was satisfying and simple: pour a ladleful of batter on the hotplate, and when the surface starts to firm, flip the pancake. The chalkboard menu offered just three fillings—traditional lemon and sugar, chocolate sauce, mashed banana.

Three things occurred to her as she made her first pancake. The memory's clear as day. One: there's no high-value food wastage in making pancakes—that's a kill factor for any catering business. Two: the beach bar could charge more if they wiped *Pancakes* off the menu board and chalked up *Crêpes*. Three: if *she* owned the bar, she'd offer savoury fillings too—*Galettes*. People pay more for a savoury snack; it's closer to a proper meal. She now recognizes that these observations—made while the batter bubbles popped on the hotplate—constituted an *instinctive entrepreneurial insight*.

The problem Freya faced back then was twofold: no savings, and no prospect of ever having business premises. Fast-forward to last summer: Freya was chatting with old Tom, who operated the chip 'n' sauce van at her local beach, and she mentioned she'd love to have a small business like his. He gave her the nod that he'd be retiring soon, and the license would be up for grabs. She went straight round to her ex-boyfriend Craig, who was by then married to the parish council clerk. Freya is good mates with both of them, partly because she makes it her business not to fall out with anyone; it's a small community. Freya told her ex she wanted the license, had saved up some money, and had written a business plan. Which she hadn't at the time, but all the figures were in her head. And she told him she'd already researched all the health and safety codes, which again she hadn't. Plenty of time to do her homework. As soon as old Tom terminated his lease, the clerk told Craig, and Craig told Freya. She prepared the best ever business plan for a street food operation, thanks to Mr. Filipkowski's library, and submitted her application.

So now she's in the proverbial chicken-and-egg situation. The parish council met last night, and there on the agenda—sooner than Freya had expected—was *Applications for the street food vendor lease.* If she's offered the lease, she'll have to prove she has the resources. That is, the money to execute her business plan: money for the monthly licence fee, a hotplate, build costs for a moveable stall, and a start-up supply of wholesale foodstuffs.

X

On the bus, she closes her eyes. Thank God. Thank God Almighty. Gerard has messaged her: *Sorry for the delay. I've been travelling. Money transferred. Don't spend it all at once.* Freya doubts his reason for the delay. But that doesn't matter. She could go out tomorrow and buy a second-hand chalet, a newish one, on a residential park. But she won't. Business comes first.

X

Freya steps off the bus, spots Skye running towards her across the beach. Her eyes mist—he watched out for her. Behind Skye, there's a deranged game of football in progress, and Freya sees Skye's friend Billy. He kicks the ball high into the air; the wind whips it away. On dry days, she and Skye meet here at the end of her shift. His first question is invariably,

"Any food?" So Freya is already pulling the salmon sandwich from her pocket. But today he shouts, "Heard anything, Mum?" He reaches her, red-faced and sweaty.

She shakes her head. "Not yet. The clerk might be writing to me at this very minute. But I guess there's more important stuff to deal with, planning applications, that kind of thing."

He takes the sandwich from her outstretched hand, and without checking the filling, he takes a mouthful. "I haven't told anyone. Promise."

"Don't speak with your mouth full." He rolls his eyes at her. "Once I hear, Skye, you can tell anyone you like."

"And you're sure you'll get it?"

"Can't be sure, my lovely, but most of the councillors know me. They know I'll work hard. Why do you think I organized the beach litter-pick last week?"

They sit cross-legged, side by side on the sand. "I hope you get it, Mum. You'd be here by the beach all through the summer while I'm playing." He looks up at her. "Will me and my friends get free pancakes?"

She laughs. "All you think about is food. Go on, join the others for ten minutes. Then we'll go back to the chalet."

Skye runs full pelt towards his friends, and sharply changes direction as the ball is kicked across the beach. Freya's reminded that the boy's sportiness doesn't come from her. It definitely comes from his father—a good-looking surfer boy when she met him. Broad-shouldered, hair bleached by the summer sun. He had all the charm you'd expect from a fancy upbringing. No dropped consonants. An IVF upgrade if she ever met one.

That's why she kept the baby, kept Skye. It wasn't part of some premeditated plan. Given that she found herself pregnant, she knew the kid would have a good start—excellent stock and so on. She decided, *now or never*. And she wasn't, and still isn't, looking for a long-term partner—a happy-family scenario. Not after her childhood. She's been happy with summertime hook-ups; they're uncomplicated. Craig was an exception, but that lasted only a couple of years. She couldn't get the hang of having another adult around—took too much effort.

"Damn," she says. She still hasn't done it. Gerard had pressed her to make a will. He insisted she acknowledge that he was Skye's father—which surprised her—even if she appointed someone else as his legal guardian. He asked, "What's going to happen to Skye if you fall off a cliff next week?" She didn't like to admit she had no disaster plan. However, she and Craig had one time agreed that he'd look out for Skye, "if anything happened." She needs to have a proper chat with him.

She stands up and tries to capture Skye's attention. One day she'll have to tell him that Gerard's his dad. For the time being, he doesn't need to know, and he doesn't need to know about the money. She'll say she's been saving up her tips.

X

Their chalet has subsided by six inches along one side, but it's more noticeable on the outside than inside. Fortunately, the slope favours the drain outlet in the shower tray. Freya gives Skye the key; he knows the routine. He'll go home and entertain himself for half an hour while she cleans the site's bathroom facilities.

Though mid-season started two weeks ago, the campsite is half-full. At one time, the site was packed through low, middle and high. Some of the stalwarts haven't returned this year, and the reason is pretty obvious to Freya. The entrance signs are bleached of colour. Half the reception notices are out of date. The open areas of grass need reseeding. And there's only so much Freya can do to spruce up the bathroom facilities. No one can fault the cleanliness, but the place needs gutting and refitting. According to *How to Build a Business Empire on One Good Idea*, once you've found success, you need to reinvest. You must refresh your business offering or else, before you know it, someone will steal your market share. You'll have no one to blame but yourself.

⚹

She clears the table as she would in the restaurant before serving dessert. She removes the salt and pepper pots and the sauce bottle, wipes crumbs off the table surface. She brings two tangerines to the table, each on a small plate. "I've been thinking, Skye. I've been saving my tips, and I feel I should spend a bit of money on your education."

If she'd cartwheeled across the kitchen, he couldn't look more surprised. "I'm serious, Skye. I think some key skills would be invaluable. How about some advanced surfing instruction with Craig's sister? She runs summer classes from Fistral Beach. And I think you could make a start towards lifeguard qualifications—improve your swimming. And what about some guitar lessons?"

He shrugs his shoulders, "Okay."

"And if I start the crêperie, and assuming all goes well, we'll think about one of those new wetsuits."

Freya has a long-term strategy which doesn't exactly fit with Gerard's idea of education. Skye has a sweet singing voice, and if he takes up the guitar, he could play the bars when he's older. And if he takes up surfing more seriously, he could easily help out Craig's sister as a summer job. Down the line, he could start his own surfing school if she buys him a few boards and wetsuits. Or, if the crêperie does a roaring trade, she could expand to other beaches. Skye could help her, join her as a business partner. From the outset of any business venture, the smartest entrepreneurs will plan their exits, according to *Smart Moves for First-Time Entrepreneurs*. Find a successor, sell your stake, retire.

She won't try to explain her strategy to Gerard. As she sees it, there's little point in Skye studying hard. It's anyone's guess which occupations will exist in ten years' time. Small-scale tourism is the safe bet around here.

�֎

For once, Freya wakes before her alarm. She sits up and gently pulls the cord by the window, raising the blind slowly so that the mechanism's click-click-click doesn't wake Skye in the bedroom next door. She gazes across the campsite towards the reception hut. Two blackbirds, a she and a he, are playing follow-my-leader. Freya soaks up the postdawn stillness, and a welcome calm settles over her. Her night's sleep was wrecked by bad dreams. She lies back with her arms behind her head and marvels at the novelty of having time to kill. She notices a spotting of mould in the top corner of her room—the corner that takes the full brunt of the westerlies.

It's her own fault she slept badly. Before she readied herself for bed, she scribbled a list of questions she should ask the council: *Ask for a longer lease than they offer. A grace period on the rent. An extension of opening hours.* And then she wrote a second time: *A longer lease.* The repetition was accidental—she wasn't trying to emphasize the point. But it caused Freya to reel as she experienced a flashback to the incessant rewriting of her confessional statement.

She sometimes wonders if she was brainwashed during her three months in the correctional unit; she hasn't touched alcohol since her incarceration. She hadn't argued with the instructor during her first re-education lesson—drinking alcohol *was* bad for pregnant women. She accepted she'd been stupid. But that wasn't enough for them. They wanted self-examination, from every angle. What she was thinking in the moment she accepted the bottle of beer? How she did she feel as she took the first swig? How did she feel as she drained the bottle? What was the scale of her regret when the police arrived? And when she entered her cell? Was her own childhood a possible cause for her transgression?

What were her self-diagnosed personality flaws? Writing, writing, more writing. She had to demonstrate self-loathing, it seemed, before they attempted to fix her. She felt they were mashing her brain.

Physically, though, the unit was comfortable, even snug. Each woman had her own cell, all identical with lime-green bedding and deep blue cushions. More like a room in a budget hotel—clean, functional, light. And no mould.

In her dream last night, she sat at a lime-green desk and scratched a story with a steel nail into the desk itself. A story about twins, a good twin and a bad twin. She kept scratching out and then rescratching the story because it didn't make any sense that the twins could be so different. When she woke up, she had pins and needles in her writing hand.

✕

She's chopping apples for breakfast when she murmurs, "Miss Trevaskis." She hopes that one day the correctional unit and Trevaskis, the warder on her wing, will completely fade from memory. It doesn't help that Trevaskis came into the beach bar, the one with the pancake maker, during Freya's second week in the job. Freya heard her before she saw her. As warders went, she hadn't been so bad, but Freya didn't care for her motivational methods: "You've given your child the worst possible start in life. It's time to clean up your act."

At the beach bar, as soon as she heard Trevaskis, Freya took off her apron, ready to walk out on the job. But she knew if she dumped the job so soon, word would get around town. She needed a clean work record, for Skye's sake. Instead, Freya walked straight up to Trevaskis's table—she'd come in with two girlfriends—and said, "What are we having today, my lovelies?"

Trevaskis looked up, and without so much as a blink, she said, "How's it going, Freya?"

"Just fine," she replied. "Couldn't be better, thank you." And that was that. She took their order, served the drinks. Freya worked there for two years, but she didn't see Trevaskis again. A decent tipper, though: five on twenty-three.

At six o'clock on the dot, Freya lays the table for Skye's breakfast. She then slips out of the chalet, makes her way across the site to the shower block and begins the morning routine. Empty the bins, spray and mop the floors, wipe down the sinks, polish the mirrors, and finally she approaches the toilets. She doesn't mind the job, not really.

Last winter, overlooking the Gannel in Mr. Filipkowski's mansion, Freya read *Lucky Breaks of the Super Successful*. The author tried to offer encouragement—stating that a single stroke of good luck is oftentimes all it takes for a person to fulfil their true potential. But Freya knew it was a lie. It made her angry. The author seemed to imply that all her years of hard work weren't necessary, that she was a fool to imagine she could make her own luck, *make* it happen. She tore that particular page out of the book and flushed it down Mr. Filipkowski's downstairs toilet.

The message from the council clerk pings an alert as Freya is scouring a stubborn excrement mark. She stops, leaves the toilet brush standing in the toilet, and stands up straight. She peels back her plastic glove to reveal her wristband. She scans for the key, vital information: . . . *pleased to inform you . . .*

She fist pumps inside the cubicle. *"Yes. Yes. Yes."*

Phase two of her business plan is primed. There's nothing to stop her now.

But first, she returns to the toilet bowl. She scours, flushes and moves on to the next cubicle. Because Mr. Filipkowski's book, *Smart Moves for First-Time Entrepreneurs*, is emphatic on the matter of financial risk: *Don't give up the day job until the profits are rolling in.*

THE POLES OF INACCESSIBILITY

"Now listen. Don't go haring off when the train pulls into Ürümqi," says Marco. "A droid will come here to the carriage, so *stay put* until she arrives. She'll arrange for porters to transfer your bags to the next train, and she'll stay with you for the rest of the journey and while you're in Xi'an." He wags a finger at Toni. "Don't go wandering off without the droid, Mum."

She replies with a raised eyebrow: No need for all this fussing.

"We're travelling light. We really don't need porters," says Atticus. "But thanks anyway." They hug one another. The onboard public address system sounds a brief alarm and then: "Carriage doors will close in five minutes. Please leave the train if you are not travelling today on the Silk Route via Kiev, Volgograd and Astana to Ürümqi, where all passengers will change for onward destinations in China."

"Off, off, Marco, or you'll be coming with us," says Toni.

He leans over and kisses her on both cheeks. "Have fun," he says. He turns to leave, stops at the doorway to their sleeper suite and twists around. "You can't charge around like you used to. I'll be checking your health stats every day. And if I see anything untoward, I'll insist you take a day's rest. You know, *I'd* be daunted by this trip." He allows himself a smile. "Report in every day. We'll be worried sick otherwise."

Toni looks away, sees Amelie and the boys waving from the platform, and waves back. She doesn't want *anyone* worrying about her; she rejects the role of ageing relative—a nuisance factor, a distraction from younger people's busy lives. It's such a drag being a family elder. But, as Atticus says, it comes to everyone.

Well, not everyone. Her dad's been dead forty years, and her mum . . . Toni wishes she and her mum could have averaged their lifespans. Eighty years would have been a decent innings.

Of late, she finds it difficult to picture her mother; she depends on photographs. Her memories are fine threads, twisted together and stretched to the point of snapping. Eighty years—certainly ninety years—is enough for anyone. The fact is, she's even forgetting Marco as a child, feels sad seeing him as an old man.

She waves once again to her great-grandchildren. Seb's almost a teenager, and as similar to Amelie as Theo is different. Toni wishes Amelie hadn't done that; she went too far.

Just once, Toni mentioned her embarrassment over Theo's appearance to Marco. He said, "Whatever you or I think, it's nothing to do with us. It was Amelie's decision. And there's no going back." Even so, Toni feels out of phase, as though she has lived too long.

"Looks like a party on the platform," says Atticus. He sticks his tongue out at the children. "Quite a send-off, isn't it?"

Initially, they expected only Marco to come with them to St. Pancras station, but Amelie decided last weekend that she'd come along, with the boys—she wants them to feel involved with Gr'Atticus and Nan Toni's big adventure.

The public address system announces: "Doors closing in one minute. Please leave the train immediately if you are not travelling on the Silk Route today."

Toni's heart pounds, but she's not sure why. It's only a short trip. They'll have one night on the train, ten days around China, and one night on the train coming home. Probably it's the fuss they're all making—three generations waving them off. That must be it. She feels dizzy momentarily, unsure if the train is moving or if she's falling. She attempts to blow a kiss, and by the time her dizziness has faded, the train has left the platform behind.

Atticus leans back and sighs heavily. "I'm bushed! How about you?"

She nods. "It's been hectic. I'm glad Amelie came along."

"And the kids," he says.

"Yes, and the kids." His eyes look heavy to her. "Atticus, why don't you have forty winks. I'll wake you when we're in France." She sends a message to Amelie: *Thrilled you came to the station. Don't work too hard. Are you getting to bed early enough? You looked a little tired. Nan Toni xxx.*

She hopes for a quick response. Here it is: *Nothing gets past you! I'll be fine when we've shipped the current job. It's a stinker. Have a great trip and don't you dare worry about me. Amelie xxxxx.*

Toni knows her dad would be proud of Amelie following almost exactly in his footsteps—conserving paintings rather than copying them. Amelie says many of the skills are essentially the same. The train accelerates, enters a succession of tunnels under the city and, several minutes later, emerges into the Kent countryside. Atticus is asleep already.

She's confident, in a pessimistic sense, that this will be her swan-song holiday. Even with all the assisted-living tech, she finds each day an effort. She now craves familiar places, as though there's only time to reimprint good memories. She can pinpoint the best times of her life, the places where she experienced those heightened, feeling-alive moments. And there's a pleasure in returning to recapture them. But she decided long ago, on her centenary birthday, that it was high time she cast off her past, her own history, let it all slip away. She has, at last, consigned her life's milestones to a set of short, depleted sentences: *My mother died in a car accident; my father remarried; I got on well with my stepmother;* and more recently, *Millie Dack was my lifelong friend.* She feels unmoored, drifting free.

It's over a year since Millie's funeral. Her boy, Rudy, dropped by their house yesterday evening. He hadn't warned them, and in retrospect, Toni can see that he'd probably had second thoughts even as he knocked on the door. As Rudy sat down at their kitchen table, she felt a wave of guilt; she hadn't contacted him since the funeral—Millie would be disappointed in her.

Atticus opened a bottle of Bordeaux while Rudy apologized for the inconvenience—the table was untidy with medications and paperwork for their holiday. Rudy asked if they could do him a favour, a big favour, while they were away. He explained that although he'd scattered most of his mother's ashes a year ago, he'd held some back because in her will she'd requested that some of her ashes be released on distant shores and hills.

Toni said, "You're kidding!" Rudy pulled from his pocket a small metal flask, pushed it across the table. Toni said, "Don't you and your family want to do this, Rudy?"

He said, "Honestly? I think she'd prefer to go with you."

So the small canister is packed away in Toni's suitcase. As an afterthought, she packed a miniature trowel, because she had an inkling she'd inter some ashes under a blossom tree.

※

They're underground again, in Blue Bell Hill tunnel—the last tunnel this side of the Channel—and Toni's mood lifts. It's a relief to leave family and friends behind, to be with Atticus with no one else to consider. She can place her worries in a casket and shut the lid while she's out of the country.

Over recent weeks, she has obsessed about Amelie's kids. And though this worrying serves no purpose, she can't shed the feeling that she should have intervened—Amelie tends to listen to her. She still feels Amelie was wrong to have one child naturally and one child by clinic gestation. Basically, unfair. In fact, her decision to carry Seb was a clear case of misplaced sentimentality. All those damned Madonna and child paintings in her house.

Amelie convinced Nathen and the wider family that she could carry her pregnancy without any problem; at the time, her work at the museum was solitary—she didn't meet the public, she could avoid the patrons' monthly visit. But Amelie's journey to work every day proved another matter—the withering glances started to get her down. She came home in tears one day after a woman, bold as brass, told her, "If you can afford that bracelet, you can afford to look after your child better." That's when Amelie decided to take a career break. She stayed home for the rest of the pregnancy, rarely venturing out of the house, depending on Nathen to negotiate with the outside world.

But Toni is convinced that Amelie and her husband went over-board with their second pregnancy. Why did they mess with his appearance so much? He doesn't look like either of them. It's as though a neighbour's child absentmindedly wandered into their home and took up residence.

Toni tells herself she won't stress about the family from the moment the train enters the Channel Tunnel, which allows her ten minutes more to chew things over. Maybe she should double her efforts with little Theo, draw him in closer and try to ignore his delicate Pre-Raphaelite looks, his tumbling curls. Amelie really should think about a proper haircut for the boy. It's shorter than it used to be, but heavens, it looks like a knife-and-fork job.

X

Atticus wishes that Marco hadn't arranged the droid guides for their stay in China: one for Xi'an, the second for Shanghai. He and Toni sit in their carriage at the Ürümqi terminus—they've waited for ten minutes already, while all the other passengers have transferred to their onward trains. It's such an unedifying end to an awe-inspiring journey across the Eurasian steppe, across Ukraine and Kazakhstan—one that kindled in Atticus a true sense of traversing the globe. Many travellers consider the steppes a bore, but for Atticus the bore is waiting for the droid to appear. They could have transferred themselves to the Xi'an train and arranged to meet the guide at their hotel. He says, "We aren't feeble. Marco shouldn't interfere so much."

"There's no rush, Atticus. If she doesn't arrive in the next five minutes, we'll go without her and tell Marco to inform the hire company. He's only trying to help."

He pushes his face up against the window. "Wait, I think that's her. Yes, she's coming to our carriage. There's a porter too."

He turns, and his irritation fades—Toni looks calm, open-faced. She's seemed preoccupied in recent weeks, and he's determined to find out what's bothering her. He thought she might be slipping into a depression because of Millie's death, delayed grieving and so on. He suggested as much to Toni. But she insisted she didn't need any medication—said what she needed was a change of scene, that she felt jaded. And perhaps that's all there is to it, because she seems a different person today.

The female droid, pinch-waisted, appears at their carriage entrance. She's dressed in the hire company's sky-blue and yellow livery with a polka-dot neckerchief knotted jauntily off-centre. She salutes and smiles. "Welcome to Ürümqi. I'm sorry. I'm late due to circumstances beyond my control, and you will receive compensation. I will look after you for your onward train journey to Xi'an and guide you during your tour of the city. Please tell me if you'd prefer to be addressed formally or informally."

Atticus says, "Informally, please. Old Git One"—he points to Toni, then opens his hands—"and Old Git Two. You may abbreviate: OG One and OG Two."

Toni rolls her eyes. "I'll overrule that if I may. I'm Toni, and he's Atticus."

The droid dips her head. "You may call me LanBo or Blue Wave." She stands aside, allowing the porter to shuffle in and take their baggage. "Let's go," she says breezily, gesturing the way with her hand. "You will adore Xi'an. Have you been there before? I can arrange the full tour of the five terracotta warrior sites and—"

Toni says, "No, please don't. We'd like to spend our time walking the walls of Xi'an city. We've seen the warriors three times over the last, let's see . . . eighty-odd years."

Blue Wave brings her palms together as if in prayer. "You have made a very good choice. Xi'an's fortifications are the best preserved in China."

And the walls will be an auspicious place to scatter Millie's ashes to the wind.

⋇

The next day, they take the hotel's courtesy pod with Blue Wave to Xi'an's city walls. At Yongning Gate, they take an escalator to the top. There's something so relaxing, Toni feels, about returning to a place that you've already photographed and recorded. During Toni's journo days in China, she often made mention of this city—the blossom gardens around the fortifications, the discordant views of old Xi'an *inside* the walls and new Xi'an *outside*, and the street food vendors who operate near all the major road junctions. This is one of her favourite places.

She strides out onto the wide bricked path. She counts. It takes ten paces to reach the middle. She looks in one direction, turns and looks in the other. The path stretches into the far distance. Flags and red lanterns hang from black poles positioned every hundred metres along the wall. Younger visitors are riding bicycles; some things never change. Blue Wave is already streaming off facts and figures—the number of watchtowers, armouries—but Toni hasn't come here to be educated. She hasn't told Atticus, but she feels an overwhelming sense of calm here. It's the permanence; she adores the brickmaker's marks—carved into the original bricks, still sharp.

Blue Wave points in the direction of the distant gatehouse. "We have a new attraction. Look. Please don't be frightened."

They see a shimmering. Tourists in the distance appear to move aside. As the shimmering effect dampens and seemingly solidifies, Toni and Atticus see the warriors. "There must be hundreds!" says Atticus.

"Exactly one thousand holo-form warriors. Stay where you are. They will detect you and march around you," says Blue Wave.

Atticus and Toni walk forward and instinctively separate. At a distance of one hundred metres, the single-hued terracotta warriors morph into full colour—each face as real as any flesh-and-blood human. They quicken from a marching pace, unsheathe their swords in an instant and gather speed to a crouching run. Silent and ghostlike. Toni imagines a guttural roar.

Eight abreast, the warriors charge past. Toni finds herself isolated. She can't see Atticus. She faces wave upon wave of armour-clad warriors. She sees light ahead and realizes she's holding her breath. Three lance bearers bring up the rear. They jog with spears held at shoulder height, seemingly relaxed. But they lengthen their strides in unison, arch backwards and hurl their spears. Toni jerks back, her forearms reaching her chest as a spear flies through her and beyond. She freezes as the spear bearers run past.

Hearing giggles, she looks back. Two young children raise their hands to conceal their glee, but their small bodies shudder with silent laughter. They're totally unfazed by the warriors.

Atticus puts his arm around her shoulders. "I can think of worse ways to go—a spear through the throat. You know, I've often thought that I'd prefer to die in a fight—like a street fight—than die in my sleep. I can't imagine anything worse than simply not waking up. At least in a fight, you know that death is imminent."

Toni takes a breath. "If you're serious, Atticus," she says, "I'll make arrangements."

)(

In the Long Bar of the Waldorf Astoria in Shanghai, Atticus is writing a list. It's a list for Rudy of all the places where they sprinkled Millie's ashes. He assumed Toni would be keeping a record—it's a Munroe-family thing after all, making lists—but she asked *him* to write it all down. He hopes that after seven wonderful, carefree days together, she isn't taking a morbid turn. It wouldn't be surprising—carrying Millie's ashes around all week. His mild disappointment with the holiday is that Toni has visited *only* her old haunts, as though she's saying to herself, One last time. He'd prefer to see new places; there's no need for their adventures to stop.

Atticus cancelled the droid hire for Shanghai; he doesn't trust them. They're cheap for a reason. They push sponsored events, hurry you through your own schedule so they can shepherd you to an exhibition you're not interested in, take a contorted route past specific advertising sites. They must think people are gullible.

The waiter brings their order—two white chocolate mochas. It's a reminiscence for Toni. She came here as a teenager with her dad, and this is the drink she ordered. Atticus is incredulous that Toni remembers such detail. It seems her memories of that visit are scribed in neon.

Toni chortles. "I don't think Rudy will expect grid references, Atticus." He's relieved; she's okay. "Don't forget the park opposite our hotel in Xi'an. I placed a pinch of ashes under a bonsai."

He adds this to the list, which already includes:

The gardens at the base of Xi'an city walls, near the An'ding Gate.
In the Huangpu River by the Bund, opposite the Waldorf Astoria.
In the People's Park in Shanghai, where Toni took her Tai Chi classes.
In West Lake in Hangzhou—under a peach tree on Su Causeway.

"I've saved a spoonful for our trip tomorrow," says Toni.

〤

This is Suzhou, the Venice of the East, twenty minutes by bullet train from Shanghai. Toni and Atticus set out from their hotel on Shiquan Street in the old town and turn down the cobbled alleyway, which leads to the Master of the Nets Garden. The alleyway takes them through a dense, low-rise residential area and opens out into a high-walled courtyard. On the left side of this courtyard stands the imposing wooden gateway to the garden. Immense doors are pushed inwards into a dark entrance hall, and there's a glimpse of the garden beyond. Toni has always stated, categorically, that this is her favourite place on earth. With a rush of adrenaline, and the fluidity of a woman thirty years her junior, she walks towards a fairy-tale vista—craggy limestone rockeries, blossom trees and pavilions set around the Rosy Cloud Pool.

"When I came here with Dad, I imagined a zombie horde trying to scale the walls. I imagined that this walled garden was the last safe place in Suzhou, and the Master of the Nets was the sole survivor of a zombie apocalypse. And you know the three bamboo paintings? I took the original photos here—Dad made the painted copies back in London." Atticus knows the story of the bamboo paintings, but the zombie horde is an embellishment he hasn't heard before. Toni can still surprise him.

They cross a zigzag stone bridge towards the Waterside Pavilion of Washing Hat Ribbons. They sit together by a limestone outcrop and hold hands. The tops of the tallest cherry trees are tousled by a stiff breeze, but the air is barely disturbed within the garden.

"You know, Atticus, I told Millie about the gardens in Suzhou—this one, the Humble Administrator's Garden and the gardens at Tiger Hill. I nearly persuaded her to come here after Julia was born. She was so unhappy for a while back then."

"I didn't know that."

"You were away from home around that time. I think you had a new love interest." She looks at him and smiles as she pats his hand. "Or maybe Millie asked me not to tell you. I can't remember now. She'd had a fallout with Rudy. Well, you know how it is after a birth—everyone's emotional and exhausted. Things were said that couldn't be unsaid, if you see what I mean. Took her a long time to recover."

"She should have come here. She'd have loved it. I never understood why she was so timid."

"Yes, timid about travel. Personally, I blame her parents; they were so overbearing. Millie said the strangest thing to me one time. She said she used to fantasize as a child about being brought up by another family. She'd look at other families in the street and say to herself, They'd be better than my parents." They fall silent for a while. "But she loved her sister. So that's something."

Toni opens her sling bag and removes the metal canister. "Let's follow the path, find somewhere quieter." The path is inlaid with pebble mosaics of fish and chrysanthemums. They pass through a circular opening into the simplest of gardens—a singular smooth boulder set below a purple magnolia tree. And onwards, they find the Meditation Study with its fretted exterior panels and a small courtyard planted with bamboo. A woman is sweeping the entrance, and she wanders away as Toni and Atticus approach.

"Let's do it now. Stand over there, Atticus, and tell me if anyone's coming." With difficulty, even with her exo-skel, Toni crouches down by the bamboo. She opens the capsule, pours the remaining few ashes onto the freshly turned soil, and draws the miniature trowel from her bag. She works the soil and ashes together.

❈

Toni suggests, as they board the Silk Route train heading westwards, that they book an early lunch in the dining car. "The view will be better than in our suite," she says.

"Good idea. You make the booking, and I'll send a message to Marco—tell him we're on board."

She suddenly feels the urge to disembark. Over the course of the past week, she's felt herself becoming more like Millie: reticent. Yesterday, she demurred when Atticus suggested a day trip outside Shanghai to Pingshan, a village with classic Huizhou architecture—a place they've never been before. Having visited all her favourite places, she didn't want to risk ending their trip on a potentially disappointing note. But Atticus was right to make the suggestion, and she felt bad he wouldn't go there without her.

They savour their light lunch of jianbing, a spiced Chinese version of crêpes, with spring onion, coriander and egg. Toni asked for a jianbing without mustard tubers, and Atticus warned, "Go easy on the chilli."

"I'll miss the food," says Toni. "I hope we'll be back sometime soon."

The waiter brings their coffee. He asks, "Have you enjoyed your stay in China?" They say they have. Toni asks where he's from, and he says he lives in a village called Turpan, south of Ürümqi on the old Silk Road. Toni knows that the word *village* doesn't translate; the waiter is referring to a town, of probably half a million souls. The waiter says that people call Turpan "a place as hot as fire"; it is famous for its hot sand baths and its mountains, which appear to be aflame. He says Turpan is the most beautiful place in the whole world, and they should visit *now* because it's the very best time—not too hot and not too cold.

When the waiter moves on to the next table, Atticus says, "Sounds wonderful, doesn't it?" He pushes. "Don't you think?" And pushes again. "We never did visit Ürümqi or explore Xinjiang Province. It didn't reach the top of the list, did it?"

"It was horribly polluted when we lived here. We couldn't have taken Marco."

"I've always fancied getting off the train at Ürümqi. You know, I first heard about Ürümqi in school in geography lessons. It's near one of the poles of inaccessibility."

Toni grimaces. "What?"

"Ürümqi is close to the Eurasian pole of inaccessibility—the farthest point on the Eurasian land mass from a coastline. Just as . . . the town of Allen in North Dakota is North America's pole of inaccessibility." He laughs, "See, occasionally I know stuff you don't."

"I didn't realize geographers could be so poetic. It's lovely: a pole of inaccessibility. Maybe I should write an article . . ."

"Why not?"

A second waiter passes through the carriage, offering a choice of liqueurs. Toni and Atticus decline the spirits, but after conferring—they agree they can nap after lunch—they ask for two small glasses of tawny port. As the waiter pours, Toni says to Atticus, "Millie developed a taste for port. I'd pick up a bottle, something unusual, when I was travelling."

In her mind's eye, Toni sees Millie in her armchair, a generous measure of port in hand, invariably in the same etched glass. She sees Millie studying her projected maps, timetables for shipping routes and train journeys, timelines of political alliances and trading agreements. "Millie called it a marriage made in heaven, you know—England and Portugal, *their* wine and cork traded for *our* cod. She had a brilliant talent for summary. Part of a civil servant's job, I suppose." She smiles, and her eyes mist. "Here we are on the Silk Route, and Millie probably knew all the history of trade in this part of the world. It's a crying shame she never made this journey."

But Toni wonders if Atticus is listening at all, if his thoughts are still at the poles. Indeed, he continues: "Let's see. In South America, the pole of inaccessibility is near Arenápolis in Brazil—never been there. In Australia, it's near Papunya in the Northern Territory—haven't been there either. And in Africa, the pole is somewhere near the borders of . . . I can't remember, but it's close to a town called Obo. I remember that much. And I always thought, as a kid, I'd travel to all the poles in my lifetime."

Toni falls quiet, gazes out at a stony desert that stretches north to the Gobi and Mongolia. "You know, Atticus," she says without looking at him, "there must be thousands of people our age in Turpan who haven't ventured outside their province, or even outside their own valley. And look at how many places we've seen and explored." She isn't sure Atticus heard this either. He's looking out of the window too. He's probably disappointed in her. But she *has* been intrepid for most of her life; she set the pace for so many years. Imagine if he'd married Millie—talk about total opposites. They'd have split years ago. Toni grins.

"What's tickling you?" Atticus asks.

"Oh, I was just thinking about Millie."

She wonders what her old friend might say if she were still alive. If she could whisper in Toni's ear, right now . . . She smiles, for she hears Millie's voice: *Get off the train, will you? Go and explore. Come home and tell me everything.*

ACKNOWLEDGMENTS

Dreams Before the Start of Time started out, three years ago, as a short, novella-length manuscript. My editor at 47North, Jason Kirk, encouraged me to revisit and expand that work. Thank you, Jason, for your excellent advice—from that initial prompt through to the novel's completion.

My thanks also to Garry, Rob and Adam, always my first readers. And thanks are also due to Alex Jungwirth for her advice when I visited China.

As ever, many thanks to the delightful and diligent team at 47North.

It's my pleasure to thank Dr. Aarathi Prasad for our conversation about human reproductive technologies. Aarathi's astonishing book *Like A Virgin: How Science Is Redesigning the Rules of Sex* formed the starting point for my research. I may have occasionally misinterpreted my research sources, or added embellishments for fictional purposes. For the former, I apologize.

I refer to a number of paintings in this novel:

A Goodnight Hug, 1880, Mary Cassatt, pastel on paper.

The Boating Party, 1893–1894, Mary Cassatt, oil on canvas.

Seaport with the Embarkation of the Queen of Sheba, 1648, Claude (also known as Claude Lorrain), oil on canvas.

Madonna of the Meadow, 1505–1506, Raphael, oil on board.

Christ in the Carpenter's Shop; or, Christ in the House of His Parents, 1849–50, John Everett Millais, oil on canvas.

The Last of England, 1852–1855, Ford Madox Brown, oil on panel.

You will find images on my Pinterest page: www.pinterest.com/annecharnock.

Chapter 8, "The Adoption," in a slightly different form, was first published in an anthology titled *Phantasma*, edited by J. D. Horn and Roberta Trahan.

ABOUT THE AUTHOR

Photo © Yvette Owen

Anne Charnock's writing career began in journalism. Her articles appeared in the *Guardian*, *New Scientist*, *International Herald Tribune* and *Geographical*. Her debut novel, *A Calculated Life*, was a finalist for the 2013 Philip K. Dick Award and the 2013 Kitschies Golden Tentacle Award. Her second novel, *Sleeping Embers of an Ordinary Mind*, was included in the *Guardian's* "Best science fiction and fantasy books of 2015." Learn more at www.annecharnock.com, on Twitter @annecharnock, and on Pinterest at www.pinterest.com/annecharnock.